A FAREWELL TO CHARMS

MOLLY HARPER

A Farewell to Charms
Copyright © 2021 by Molly Harper
Ebook ISBN: 9781641972314
KDP ISBN: 9798848552348
IS POD ISBN: 9781641972369

NYLA Publishing
121 W 27th St., Suite 1201, New York, NY 10001
http://www.nyliterary.com

A FAREWELL TO CHARMS

1

ALEX

ALEX LANCASTER WAS a man accustomed to being in control. He was a man accustomed to the world aligning itself around him in an orderly fashion, allowing him to do what he wanted when he wanted. He was not accustomed to sitting on the side of the road in a place called the Devil's Armpit, sweating through his suit as he stared into a smoking engine, inhaling what smelled like a combination of deviled egg farts and feet.

"Move to Mystic Bayou, they said. An exciting career opportunity, they said. Complete control over an entire special division, they said. Well, they didn't say anything about the Devil's Armpit! Ow, shit!" Alex hissed in pain as his hand made contact with some burning hot engine part. He jerked back and knocked into the metal leg holding up the hood, which slammed shut. It just barely missed his fingertips.

Alex shook his hands out, grateful that while they were burnt, they were at least, intact. He did not need to add "inability to type/text" to his list of problems. He used his wrinkled sleeve to mop the sweat gathering on his brow. This had been a day of failure and frustrations, something that was becoming a trend in his life during the last few months. His meeting in New Orleans, an attempt to secure a direct transport line for goods and materials from the port to Mystic Bayou, had gone about as well as running a dart game in a hurricane. The town was growing, suddenly outpacing the regular deliveries of groceries, fuel, building materials, and every other modern convenience people couldn't reasonably do without.

There were construction projects all over town, including the apartment buildings meant to ease the town's housing crisis, but the only project that had been completed was an artifact storage facility at the former rift site. And that was only because Alex's boss, Darwin Messina, considered what was essentially a super-max prison for haunted antiques to be the highest possible priority. Now that the rift – an interdimensional tear that originally drew the *magique* to the bayou in the first place – was closed, the town was the perfect remote, secure place to deposit dangerous historical and/or magical items the League had collected over the years. The new apartment complex was *nearing* that level of importance, but it wasn't there yet.

Even with the League's resources and Sonja Fong's legendary organizational skills, they simply couldn't help local businesses provide enough of what the citizens needed. There were too many timelines and contingencies to contend with, not to mention the legal and financial complexities of working with small, privately owned businesses. And frankly, Alex was starting to suspect that asking truckers to cross the Devil's Armpit was a factor working against him. Who would want to do this on a regular basis? Despite offering the League's usual highly attractive compensation packages to five regional trucking contractors, Alex couldn't find a single company willing to work with them.

Alex liked to see himself as prepared for anything, but not being able to persuade *one* company to agree to work with him was simply mind-boggling. The League always had some link, some secret useful connection to create the desired outcome. The International League for Interspecies Cooperation was, at its best, a *connection* – between the world of the humans and the world of the supernatural, between different species and groups of *magique* creatures and between the various secret business interests of beings who had turned their magical gifts into successful money-making ventures. At its worst, it was a shadowy secret organization that sometimes enforced its will with an iron fist and the ruthless efficiency of a Monty Python sketch.

Still, Alex liked to think that as the executive director of the Mystic Bayou branch of the operation, he was directing the League's resources for the greater good. People were safe in Mystic Bayou from threats past and present, and they were, for the most part, happy and healthy. All he had to do was somehow provide what they needed in the middle of the town's historic population boom.

For decades, the League had prepared for the human world to discover that the creatures they told campfire tales about since the dawn of time were *real* and had been living amongst them in secret. Once the word got out thanks to a viral video of a shifter's meltdown over a parking spot, the administration hoped that they could persuade said humans that the creatures just wanted to live their lives as normal people and had no interest in eating them. (For the most part.)

What the League hadn't anticipated after the "Eustace Cornwell incident" was for the public to track down and descend upon what had always been a secret supernatural utopia.

Years before, the League sent pre-eminent anthropologist Jillian Ramsay, PhD, to interview citizens of Mystic Bayou about their unique community, where humans knowingly lived alongside the *magique*, as all otherworldly creatures were called in the Bayou, blending their lives and cultures together to create a beautiful and welcoming place to live.

Within days of the parking lot incident making headlines, Jillian's book – *The Bayou: A Wholehearted Approach to a Blended Community* – was the next thing to go viral. Though the town was never *officially* mentioned by its full name, the omission didn't stop dedicated sleuths from tracking it down. Since then, droves of curious humans had arrived in Mystic Bayou parish limits and many of them planned to stay. The enamored humans wanted to live in a place where they could see the creatures they'd read about since childhood, and the *magique* wanted a hometown tailored for them from the ground up.

This created a hydra of crises within the town. There weren't enough places to rent or buy, meaning newcomers were living in improvised campgrounds off Main Street. There weren't enough jobs to go around. There weren't enough places to buy groceries or gas. The town only had one restaurant, run by a cranky brownie who didn't appreciate gluten-free requests. The postmaster, Bonita De Los Santos, requested funding to expand the post office to accommodate the increased demand on routes and post boxes. And as more social media posts went up, more busloads of tourists poured into town, creating traffic jams and generalized chaos.

Carefully and deliberately, Alex and Sonja worked through these problems like the logistical maze they were. It amazed him that in this day of immediate gratification and lightning-fast internet (outside the Bayou, anyway), he was troubled by something as simple as finding transportation for inanimate objects. Given the uncomfortable expressions and the repetitive, almost-scripted responses he got from the contractors he'd met that afternoon, Alex suspected that the trucking companies were cooperating against him somehow, conspiring to drive up the terms of the contract. But he also thought this could be paranoia and possibly a delusion brought on by heat combined with the sulfurous stink coming off the Devil's Armpit.

Alex's League-issued SUV started acting up the moment he'd left the city proper. The temperature gauge on the engine started to climb steadily. He probably should have stopped at a station, but he'd hoped he'd be able to make it back to town before it reached the "critical" stage. And now, he wasn't sure exactly what he was supposed to do about the engine temp or the eerie *cha-plunk-cha-plunk-cha-plunk* noise it had been making. Alex had a rudimentary knowledge of cars when he'd traveled with his family on the carnival circuit, back when he called himself Alex Carver. You had to know how to patch a tire, replace a dead spark plug or even re-attach a muffler with nothing but baling wire and happy thoughts, if you wanted to keep up with the caravan. But cars were half computer now and Alex had no idea what he was looking at when he lifted the hood.

He'd thought he was safe when he'd reached the Devil's Armpit, the last geographical barrier before one crossed into the Mystic Bayou parish. But half-way through that particularly odorous landmark, the little red digital temperature needle on his dashboard suddenly shot up the last few millimeters to "HOT." And then his engine made a sound like the shriek of a wounded dolphin. He'd had just enough time to pull over to the shoulder before the car shuddered to a stop.

He was stuck. Alex Lancaster, the most trusted and capable lieutenant of Darwin Messina himself, was stranded on the side of the road like a horror movie ingenue. His cell, which he'd yet to forsake for one of Sonja's fancy satellite models, didn't pick up a signal out here. And he'd told his assistant, Jessica, that he might stay at a hotel in town if his meeting ran late. So, no one would think anything was amiss if he just didn't show up that night. His options were trying to walk the remaining twenty miles into town or sleep in his car, which would essentially turn into an oven full of stink overnight.

Alex scrubbed a hand over his face, not registering the sound of wheels crunching over gravel behind him. His father, one of the best-known menders in the business, known for his resourcefulness and adaptability in any given situation, from securing vets for sick petting zoo ponies to getting a Tilt-A-Whirl car replaced in Fairbanks, Alaska, on a *Sunday*, would be ashamed.

Why hadn't he stopped in New Orleans, stayed in a nice four-star hotel and enjoyed some room service? Why? Alex had wanted to get home, he'd told himself, as he'd put the Crescent City in his rearview. But it wasn't like he had anyone or anything waiting for him in his League-issued trailer. Hell, he didn't even have a cat. He'd been thinking about getting one, but then he'd be a single guy living with a cat, and that didn't seem fair to the cat.

How sad was it that if he disappeared overnight, absolutely no one would be affected? Sonja maybe, but between her and Jillian, they could run the office so smoothly that no one in the League headquarters would realize he was gone.

"Can I be of any help?"

He turned toward the sound of the husky voice behind him.

Fire.

Alex was blinded by the searing sunlight reflecting off the woman's hair. It made her look like some strange angel with a flaming halo. He squinted, raising his hand to shield his eyes against the glare. He shifted his gaze to the truck parked behind her, a new dark blue F-150 with Carmody and Boudreaux's logo painted on the side.

He knew the lady in question, a full two inches taller than him and broad-shouldered. She had that dewy, flushed beauty often seen on women who spent hours applying layers of powder and paint to achieve a "natural look." Her long hair was a strange mix of colors – copper, gold, chestnut, even a few strands of silver – leaving the overall impression of a molten river of bronze. It fell in messy waves around her face, framing a pair of wide, light brown eyes. Unfortunately, those eyes were shielded by a pair of aviator sunglasses, reflecting back at him Alex's damp, disheveled mess.

What was her name? Abby? Ella?

"Eva!" he blurted out. "Eva Boudreaux."

She smiled, a confused quirk tilting her full lips. "Yes, I'm Eva. And *you're* Alex. I don't think we've been officially introduced, but the girls have mentioned you a couple of times. Always in a nice way, mind you." She extended her hand, pumping his up and down with confidence. She was southern, like so many people around here, but somehow her accent was more alluring – all honey and smoked bourbon that seemed to slide along his skin as she spoke.

"Yeah, that's me. I work with your friends over at the League," Alex said.

"Are you all right?" she asked, her brows furrowing together in concern. Her voice was musical in its lilting smoothness, making the hair on his neck stand up. It was a beautiful break from the relentless, shirt-soaking heat. "It looks like the heat's gotten to ya. I have some water in my truck."

"I'm OK," he said, shaking his head. He'd been staring at her. And he was pretty sure his mouth had been hanging open. Not exactly the picture of administrative confidence. "I haven't been out here that long."

"Well, at least let me look at that engine. You wouldn't have stopped out here unless you'd had to. No one spends time in the Devil's Armpit except mosquitoes and tourists who don't know any better," Eva said.

"I'm sure it's fine," he said. "I think I can have it up and running as soon as it cools down."

Behind him, his car made a belching noise and spit out a cloud of steam that made him bolt towards her in alarm. She didn't flinch, simply grinned at him, and tied that strange molten hair up in a messy bun as she walked towards the SUV.

"Well, I'm not quite as good with cars as I am with boats, but even I can see that *this*," she paused to point her elegant, long-fingered hands at the steam billowing from under his hood, "is not fine."

He nodded silently, his eyes trailing to where her overalls were tied around a waist that took on an hourglass shape between those shapely hips and the sweetly rounded tops of her...

Alex cleared his throat and looked away. He knew he shouldn't be checking out her cleavage when she was helping him out. But when she was leaning over like that, her tank top clinging to all that smooth skin, his better judgment self-ejected into the water and was eaten by whatever monsters lived there. As she'd passed, he wondered what she smelled like, close-up. Was it wrong that he wanted to take a step nearer to find out? Probably.

Oh, good grief, was he drooling?

He quickly wiped at his chin before she noticed that he was

making a complete jerk of himself. Eva deftly flipped up the hood with one hand and peered into his engine.

"Whoo," she huffed, waving the wisps of smoke out of her face. "Well, this isn't ideal running condition, is it?"

He shook his head without making any sounds. He wasn't sure he had the air to produce any.

She bent over into the engine. No, wait, his body had chosen this unfortunate moment to connect his brain and his mouth.

"Hot," he wheezed.

"Sure is. Why don't you go get some of that water?" she called, her voice amplified by the metal hood. He followed the order, because, again, he was approaching complete-jerk territory. When he'd gulped down the better part of a chilled liter bottle, he returned to find her elbow deep in his car, moving in a brisk, surgical manner, muttering to the car like she was soothing a recalcitrant patient. She didn't even complain of her hands burning as she tapped and plucked at the engine like it was a mechanical harp.

Alex should have known the woman would be some sort of engine genius. He'd seen her around town on occasion, but he'd never gotten this close because she was usually accompanied by Jon Carmody, getting along "like a house afire," as Mayor Zed Berend put it. It was well known in the Bayou that Jon could fix any boat with any problem, and Jon had cut Eva in on his family business – a great shock to the older crowd who spent most of their day jawing over it at the local pie shop. For Jon to go so far as to rename his grandfather's repair business to include Eva, she had to have some serious talent. The pair of them were so close, if Alex hadn't known that Jon was ridiculously in love with Lia Doe, he might have suspected that Jon and Eva were a couple. But Jon and Lia were pretty public about their happiness, like a pair in one of those shrewdly sweet cable holiday romance movies. Not that Alex was bitter about it or anything, having had some pretty serious interest in Lia himself for a bit.

OK, maybe he was a little bitter about it. Lia wasn't the first woman to have left Alex flat for some local guy she'd just met in

Mystic Bayou. First, his childhood sweetheart, Cordelia Canton, had blown off any consideration of a reconciliation to take up with a sort-of dead Irish guy. Then Lia... well, to be fair, he'd only had a *brief* but intense interest in Lia, but who wouldn't? She was a lovely, lithesome mystery and she'd ditched him the minute Jon had so much as smiled at her.

What was it about these local guys? Was it that they were *magique*, all manner of enigmatic and powerful shifters? How was he supposed to compete with men who could turn into dragons or lions or, in Zed's case, a massive and frankly, fucking terrifying, bear? Or maybe it was the accent. Women seemed to love a good Southern accent, especially when the guy dropped random French words into conversation like Zed did. And Alex's lifelong efforts to polish up his diction had resulted in his sounding like a newscaster from Anywhere, Indiana.

So no, he hadn't been close enough to Eva to enjoy this sort of... what would you even call drooling on the side of the road while a beautiful woman saved your ass? Contact? Conversation? Creepery?

Eva seemed happy to simply orbit in the warmth of Jon and Lia's life, spending time with their friend circle, living next door to them and working with Jon in his boat shop. But now, Alex had a million questions he wanted to ask her and couldn't seem to find the wherewithal to ask them. Was Eva happy in the Bayou? Did she want something more or would she build her life here, like everyone else seemed determined to do? Did she realize he was staring at her beautifully curved backside as she puttered around in his engine?

He was *not* a good man.

"A-ha!" she said suddenly, straightening and brandishing a limp bit of gray plastic that was dripping onto the pavement. He wasn't sure if she'd finally burned herself or if she'd realized he was ruthlessly objectifying her as she did him a favor. He was prepared to run, either way.

"Radiator hose!" she crowed. "For all the extras they've stuffed inside cars here lately, you still need your engine cooled to keep it running. I have a couple in my truck, one of them will probably get you back to town. But you'll have to ask somebody with more experience than me to fix it long-term."

Before he could object, Eva was rummaging around in her truck for the spare part and transplanting it into his SUV. He wasn't surprised in the least when she eventually climbed into the driver's seat and the engine roared back to life as if nothing had ever been wrong. Her smile was triumphant and transfixing as she hopped out of the SUV, wiping her hands on the lilac-colored bandana she kept in her back pocket. It appeared to be printed with sweetly grinning sloths.

Curiouser and curiouser.

"I'll follow you back to town, make sure you get there safe," Eva said.

"Er, thank you." He cleared his throat, absolutely sure that his cheeks were flushed and red. It *was* a little emasculating, having a woman worrying whether he would make it home safely, but Eva was simply better at this mechanical stuff than he was. And her vehicle was in good working order while his was not. Gender had nothing to do with it.

"I'd like to pay you something, for your help. This is time you could have spent on other customers."

"Oh, I couldn't!" she exclaimed, the wattage of her smile dampening.

"But it wouldn't even come out of my pocket. The League would be paying you. We want to foster good relationships with local vendors. And we can't do that, taking advantage of unpaid labor."

Her expression was almost sad as she peered over her mirrored sunglasses at him. All at once, he had a strange feeling of being found wanting, and he wished he could explain, assure her that he wasn't a corporate douche with a calculator for a heart. He just couldn't seem to find the same easiness with the locals that everybody else seemed to have.

Or it was possible he was a corporate douche. He wasn't sure anymore. He was *so* sweaty right now.

"What about fostering good relationships between *neighbors?*" she asked. "That's part of what living in Mystic Bayou is all about, helping people because they need it – not because you could get something out of it. It's not why I came here, but it's a big piece of why I've stayed."

He cleared his throat and took another sip of the water. "You make an excellent point."

"I usually do," she told him primly, her lips quirking. "Now, get in that car and don't get too confident on the gas. She's still a little shaky."

He nodded sharply. "I'll do what I'm told."

She snorted as she pressed a hand to her broad chest. "Magical words that I've been waiting to hear all my life."

IT TOOK FOREVER to roll into Mystic Bayou, primarily because Alex refused to drive over twenty-five miles per hour on a borrowed radiator hose. It was weirdly intimidating, having her following him, knowing she was probably judging his driving and whether he was someone who listened to her sound professional advice. He didn't want to disappoint her.

Main Street was busier than usual this late in the afternoon, with people bustling around on the sidewalks, carrying groceries and carryout bags for their evening meals. Others sat around the town square, talking, eating pie from Bathtilda's and taking selfies in front of the town's now-famous fountain – paid for by the Boones – depicting all manner of supernatural creatures sheltered under a dragon's outstretched wings.

Alex didn't recognize about half of the crowd and that was... unsettling. Very quickly, he'd become accustomed to knowing his neighbors here, and he supposed Eva was right. That was part of the charm of living in such a small town, knowing the people around you. He hadn't exactly made close friends here, but... yeah, there was no way to follow up on that statement that didn't sound pathetic. The point was he'd developed a sense of whom he could trust in Mystic Bayou and whom he couldn't, and now that sense was obliterated.

With a sigh of relief, Alex parked his SUV in his usual spot near the front of the League's research village. Eva honked her horn, waving as she drove away. He found that he was strangely sad that she hadn't stopped. He could have invited her into his trailer, offered her something to drink. He wondered what she'd think of the place. The League had done their best to provide plush, livable spaces for their employees, but it still looked like a prefabricated trailer. It was far more spacious than the trailer he'd grown up in, and he'd tried to dress it up with the sort of personal touches that his mother had somehow used to make their little space a home – photos from the various places he'd lived, art he'd bought in New Orleans. But it was still a prefabricated trailer done in mostly gray and laminate.

Did he even have a beer to offer her if she'd accepted the invitation? As far as he remembered, the contents of his fridge were limited to a half-empty bottle of cabernet sauvignon and an old take-out container he wasn't brave enough to open. The cat he didn't own was very lucky not to live in those conditions.

As he watched Eva drive away, Alex noticed a black pick-up truck with heavily tinted windows pull out of a parking space near the parish hall. It very slowly turned toward the outlying areas of town, where Jon and Lia lived on Sea Cove Road. But plenty of people lived out in that direction, including Eva. And there were plenty of unfamiliar cars now that so many newcomers had arrived. It was probably just a coincidence that the black truck was following Eva out of town.

Still, Alex couldn't help a heavy feeling of dread slip through his belly as the truck's taillights disappeared into the deepening dusk.

2

———

EVA

EVA BOUDREAUX HAD TRAVELED ALL over the world in her misspent youth, but there was no place for a sunset like Mystic Bayou. Even when there was a possibility that she was being spied on by a perverted alligator shifter.

Eva sipped her stout and tilted her face toward the last dying rays of the sun. She'd found she liked the sun, very much, so much so that she'd developed a considerable tan over the years. The only time she'd been so ruddy-cheeked in her "before life" was when she worked the forges, learning how to shape gold in its roughest form, in the oldest manner possible.

Looking back at her little house on the water, Eva was grateful all over again that Bael Boone rented his uncle's old place to her. Over the years, she'd lived in hovels, cabins, miner's shacks, the occasional low-rent apartment, and finally, her beloved trailer. But this adorable little waterfront house with its tidy, open rooms and worn furnishings? This was a *home*. It had been a very long time since she'd had a home. To be honest, she wasn't sure she'd ever had one before. She'd had a place to live and a family, but she'd never quite belonged there.

She belonged here.

Eva flexed her free hand. It had felt good to poke around in

Alex Lancaster's engine. She rarely got to work with cars beyond her own beloved but ancient truck, but she liked a challenge. She was proud, not only that she'd managed to get Alex back to town unscathed, but that she'd managed to get through an interaction with him without blushing or making awkward hose-related jokes.

And they'd been *right there,* on the tip of her tongue.

Though she was aware of him – you couldn't live in Mystic Bayou without being aware of the man who oversaw the whole community for the League – she'd never spoken to Alex directly. He attended most of the community's big events and could regularly be found in the parish hall or at the pie shop, but he seemed to hold himself at a distance. He was friendly with his coworkers at the League, but not friends. She'd noticed that while Jillian and Sonja seemed cordial with him, Alex didn't get invited to the gatherings her little friend group hosted. But Eva didn't know whether that was his doing or theirs. He seemed like a nice person, but she couldn't see much under the surface, at that distance.

And when she finally got close enough to speak to him, all she could do was bluff her way through by smiling and focusing on his ailing SUV.

Thank goodness she was wearing sunglasses so he wouldn't realize how hard she was staring. Alex was, simply put, a ridiculously beautiful man. He looked like he stepped out of the pages of *Unnaturally Sharp Jawlines Quarterly*, all polish and poise and purpose. That afternoon was the first time she'd seen him remotely mussed, in her embarrassingly frequent observations of the man from afar. And even with sweat on his brow and a rumpled shirt, his eyes glowed bright and his hair shone dark gold under the sun.

Alex Lancaster was a shiny thing. And her kind just *loved* shiny things.

And in a stunning development proving just how unfair the universe was, he was so much more than a pretty surface. She'd expected "generally pleasant with good manners." She hadn't expected Alex to be funny, appreciative, and self-deprecating. He didn't even try to prove that he knew as much about engines as she did. He just stepped out of her way and let her fix it.

Sitting with her feet dangling in the water, Eva flexed her hand again. It was as wide as her mother's with the same long and capable fingers. Somehow, it didn't keep her from working on the tiny metal pieces involved in any of her interests. She was reminded of exactly how delicate Alex's features were, of the narrow width of his wrists.

There was nothing small about her, or delicate. Her hands were big. Her shoulders were broad. Her feet were longer than Jon's, for goodness's sake. She knew because they'd once mixed up their work boots. And honestly, she'd never seen anything wrong with her body. It was useful. It got things done. She was built just like everybody in her family. She was perfectly herself, comfortable in her skin and with who she was. She was not a "decorative" person. Her clothes were utilitarian, the kind of things you didn't mind staining with grease or misplaced ketchup. She never got to go to the "fun" section of the lingerie store and get some delicate whisp of lace and silk, designed to be ripped off in a passionate frenzy. Her bras were built like those metal armor cups featured on inaccurate video game armor. When Eva shopped for clothes, she reached to the back of the rack every time because that's where the large sizes were kept. The human world was simply not built for people her size.

Well, fuck the human world. She was fabulous.

But still, that nagging thought that she was definitely not the sort of woman Alex Lancaster would be interested in kept picking at the back of her brain like a steel splinter working under her skin. Why was it bothering her? When a man (or woman, frankly, Eva didn't like to limit herself) was interested in her, Eva mentally calculated to determine her own interest. If it matched, she pursued. If not, she gently let them down. And if a person was disinterested in her, she got over it and moved on. So why was she so worried about Alex?

Alex was a complication she could not afford in a life she'd already allowed to get far messier than she'd ever intended. She'd seen how Alex had looked at Lia when she'd moved to town, all wistful longing and want. Frankly, Eva couldn't blame him. She'd been similarly stunned by Lia. Eva half-considered making a play for the deer shifter herself – backing off the moment she saw how completely smitten Jon was with Lia.

But that's just not what was in Alex's eyes when he looked at Eva, and that should have been fine with her. She was prone to selecting bigger, burlier types anyway. If Zed had a brother, Eva would have climbed that fictional man like a bearded tree – but never Zed himself, who had become a close friend to Eva... and was mated to an absolute darling of a woman who could create balls of lightning with her hands. Eva wasn't about to interfere with that on any level.

Casual sex with large, exuberant men. That was her wheel-house. It worked for her. Maybe it was time for her to take a weekend closer to the Gulf Coastline, find a way to relieve some of her... tension. And if she happened to locate a non-Zed bearded tree-man, all the better.

"You have a weird look on your face that I would prefer you not explain," Jon said.

Eva startled, cursing her lack of focus, thinking about Alex. She had strength on her side, and a fair amount of indestructibility, but super senses only worked when you weren't having inappropriate thoughts about unattainable men. Super senses were funny that way.

Not for the first time, she wondered how this dark-haired merman became the best friend she'd ever had. Jon was unlike any person she'd met in all her centuries living with the humans. Reclusive and taciturn until he found common ground with her, and then he'd practically drowned her in goodwill and friendship. With Jon, she didn't have to work twice as hard to prove her skill as a mechanic. He didn't resent that she was more talented than he was in some areas. He didn't take advantage of it. He simply recognized it and offered her a portion of his family's long-held boat repair business, in return for her hard work.

"Anybody ever tell you it's rude to sneak up on people? Plus, stupid when that person has access to a variety of blunt metal objects?" she asked, eying his beer with suspicion. She loved the man like a brother, but if he brought any more IPA into her home, there would be consequences.

"Your tools are all the way back there in your truck," Jon scoffed. He gracefully dropped into a sitting position and slipped his long legs into the water next to hers.

It was strange, how easily she'd fallen into step with him. She'd always been slightly apart at home, different from her family. And here? Jon had just pulled her along into his big circle of friends, a circle he had only recently joined, after so many years isolating himself. It felt like she'd just slipped into a stream that was made for her. And when she didn't know what to say in the group, there was always someone there to ask a question or move the conversation along. They all just fit together like pieces of a puzzle, but there was room for her, too. She didn't feel like she'd just been slapped on the edge. She felt a part of things.

She gestured with her bottle to the wide-open waterfront. "You assume I don't have weapons hidden nearby. You don't know my life."

He snickered. "I like to think that's not true, but you are a woman of mystery."

Her mouth twitched, even as discomfort flared inside her. Time to change the subject. "We've talked about the beer, Jon."

"It's not my fault I can't handle that intense dark shit you and Zed like so much," he said, chin-pointing to her bottle and shuddering. "Besides, this is not just a beer. This is an invitation."

"Is it six bottles of 'take your piss-water back to your own house, because I've had a long day fixing an airboat for a jackass who kept asking if I was qualified to be handling a timing belt'?" Eva asked.

Jon groaned, spanning his hand over his face. "I knew I

shouldn't have sent you down to Percy's place on your own. He's *such* a jackass."

"Well, you did try to warn me. And you can't babysit me just because a client is a jackass. Besides, Hector's a bigger client. We needed you to finish his job first," she said, taking one of his beers and wincing as she took a sip. She shook her head and handed it back to him. "At least Percy didn't ask me if my boobs got in the way during oil changes like Balfour Boone did."

"We were right to stop working for that *particular* jackass," Jon said, taking her discarded beer bottle.

"We really should start a jackass registry," she muttered. "Or at least apply a jackass surcharge."

"It's not your worst idea," Jon said. "Let's bring it up at our weekly business meeting, but like I said, this beer is an invitation. Everybody's getting together tonight..."

"Oh, gods, are they coming here?" she gasped, glancing around for the inevitable procession of vehicles that accompanied the group. "My place is not child-proofed, Jon, and last time Dalinda set fire to Sonja's curtains with a sneeze. And they were *really nice* curtains."

He chuckled, raising his hands. "Don't worry. They're not coming here. They know you're not quite up for that, yet. Jillian and Sonja, they know the group as a whole can be a little... they can be a lot. All the same, they're getting together at our place. Something about board games and snacks, I don't know. Lia and Dani were pretty excited about it. And anything that makes Dani feel better in her condition..."

Jon paused to shudder and Eva made a sympathetic noise. Ever since Dani had become impregnated with Zed's bear-spawn, her life had become a non-stop search for the nearest receptacle to throw up in. Eva thought human morning sickness was supposed to end sometime early on in the pregnancy, but Dani continued throwing up well into her second trimester.

"So Zed is basically guilting everybody into this, huh?" Eva guessed.

"He didn't really have to but, yeah, he made the baby Dalinda eyes at us. It was deeply disturbing," Jon said.

She wanted to say that Zed couldn't possibly know how to make dragon-phoenix hybrid baby eyes in an accurate fashion, but this was Mystic Bayou. Anything was possible.

"All right, then." She stood and dusted her hands off on her jeans. "Dump your not-quite-real beer in the water. Maybe it will keep the Beasleys away."

"If anything, it would draw them in," Jon muttered, before dropping the empty bottles in her recycling bins.

"You realize that if this is a trivia-based game, Jillian will destroy us, right?" Eva asked.

Jon waggled his head while swallowing his beer then sighed. "Yeah. But there will be snacks, so there's a tradeoff."

WHILE EVA'S place was the definition of clean Scandinavian minimalism, Lia had made Jon's former bachelor pad into something out of *Better Shifter Homes and Gardens*. The Carmody residence had been a comfy, sun-bleached retreat before Lia had moved in, all well-loved denim-colored furniture and softened bits of beach glass. Lia had built on that theme with driftwood sculptures and strategically placed petrified coral. She took one of Gran Carmody's lovely blue-and-white patchwork quilts and displayed it prominently on the wall. Somehow, it was both sophisticated and cozy, and Eva was deeply afraid of the creative gleam Lia got in her eyes every time she came over to Eva's place.

The crowd greeted her with their normal enveloping warmth the moment she walked in the door. It was the sort of overwhelming noise and bustle that would have scared her into hiding in the early days. But now, she simply accepted the hugs and kisses and being handed a squealing, fire-breathing baby as if it was the most natural thing in the world. And it was. These people loved her, and for a moment she allowed herself to bask in the peaceful glow of it.

Eva *loved* this town. She loved how open and accepting everybody was with each other, even if it did make it a little difficult to maintain her assumed identity. She didn't talk about her past or her kind with the group, which she knew drove poor Jillian crazy. But anthropologist or not, Jillian was professional enough not to push (too much) when a clear boundary had been drawn. But there were so few like her, out here in the human world, that if word spread that someone like her was here in the Mystic Bayou, her family would find her in no time at all.

Jon was soon dragged into the kitchen to taste-test some sort of shrimp-based experiment Lia had come up with. Having been raised in a household with staff (pause for Eva's absolute amazement), Lia had never learned to cook and was now trying to master every Cajun recipe Zed's mother, Clarissa, could throw at her. Dani tended to stick to her more cheese-based Midwestern roots when it came to kitchen-craft. Together, they usually came up with a menu that pleased everybody's palates. But tonight, it seemed that a pale green Dani was reclined on the well-loved sofa, keeping one hand over her rounded belly.

"There's a theme to tonight's menu. 'Stuff Dani's been craving.' We're hoping it will help her keep it down," Sonja told Eva quietly, placing a platter of empanadas on the table next to dim sum, gyros and other "hand-held" foods.

"The little cub has waged war on my ability to keep anything down," Dani groaned. "But somehow, food-within-food appetizers just taste *safe*."

"Pregnancy cravings are weird like that. I threw up blue lava if I went near anything mango-flavored, but towards the end I was craving all the other tropical fruits so much Bael basically lived in the grocery store parking lot," said Jillian. She waggled a copy of *A Comprehensive History of Sewing Machines* and placed it on the end table, above Eva's work boots. Jillian was always doing that, bringing Eva books she thought she might enjoy. And since Eva was fascinated by machinery, a historical guide to sewing machines would keep her up all night like a nail-biter murder mystery.

It was nice to be understood.

"And on the lava note, we don't want to see if Dani can throw up lightning, so we're encouraging her to eat foods wrapped in other foods," Sonja whispered as she threw an arm around Eva's shoulders.

"I heard that!" Dani said, sitting up.

Eva snickered and offered Sonja a gentle squeeze in return. Sonja always smelled of expensive boutiques and office supplies, a strange combination that worked for her. Eva had been surprised that Sonja, of all people, had offered her friendship on such easy and open terms. Sonja was so *fancy*. But Eva had a wealth of skills and Sonja appreciated that in a person. Every woman here was a competent and powerful person in their own right – paired with an equally capable person. Frankly, if they ever decided to take over the League and re-order the supernatural world, Eva wasn't sure Darwin Messina could stop them.

As Dani changed position on the couch, her face went a paler shade of green, somewhere in the chartreuse family. Zed appeared in a flash, placing a frosty ginger ale in her hand and easing her back onto the cushions.

"I've got you, *Abeille*," he murmured to his fiancé, his face aglow with absolute adoration before turning his attention to the swell of her belly. "OK, kiddo, we've talked about this. Yes, it's funny to make *maman* turn different colors."

"Thanks, hon," Dani deadpanned.

Zed shrugged, all innocence, "But you've got to give her just a couple of vomit-free hours a day, all right? She will have the power to ground you when you come out of there. You keep this up, you're not going to be able to leave the house until you're in graduate school."

Rolling her eyes, Dani raised her arm and gave Eva a wave. "Yeah, I'm just going to stay here. It's my least barf-y position. Hope that's cool."

Eva put a brave face on as she blew Dani a kiss from across the room. But inside, she shuddered. She glanced down at the baby in her arms. Dalinda was awfully cute, all chubby cheeks and blond curls. And she appeared to be growing her first tooth, one very sharp tooth up at the front, that one could almost describe as a fang. And she was using that fang to gnaw on... was that a cow's shin bone?

"You are both adorable and terrifying," she informed the baby, who only grinned at her and continued her enthusiastic gnawing.

Bael approached, handing Eva a bottle of stout. "I know the chew toy seems wrong, but Will said it was the best way to keep her from gnawing through the furniture or our fingers."

Eva cast a doubtful glance at Jon's brother, Will, the best (and only) doctor in town. Will shrugged. "Sometimes, we have to improvise."

Bael sighed, letting Dalinda wrap her fingers around his... which she promptly tried to drag into her mouth for further chewing. Bael gently withdrew his endangered digit.

"The parenting books said the transition from infant to toddler would be 'difficult,'" Jillian said wearily, even as she smiled at her daughter. Bael tilted his head against his wife's and kissed her temple. "The parenting books did not prepare us."

"At least she's not venomous?" Eva offered, intending it to be some sort of comfort.

While Jillian laughed, Bael's eyes went wide. "I hadn't even considered that. Will, do you think that's possible? Will, we already have enough to deal with, with the fire and all. They won't let her into the kindergarten if she's venomous, too! Will!"

Dalinda seemed to think her father having a venom-based meltdown was hilarious and burst into giggles. The giggles turned into sneezing and suddenly, the baby's head was wreathed in a halo of blue flames.

"Yikes! I will never get used to the baby phoenix thing!" Eva yelped. Fortunately, she was one of the few people in the room who could handle Dalinda in this state without getting hurt, so she didn't drop her. But she didn't fancy having her clothes set on fire, so she held her at arm's length.

"Don't you talk about my niece that way!" Zed chastised them, before getting eye level with the baby. "Now, come on, *bebe*, put the flames away so Uncle Zed can hold you. I gotta get in my practice before our cub shows up."

Dalinda squinted as if concentrating. She passed an admirable amount of gas, and incongruously the flames died out. Zed scooped the baby out of Eva's arms. She babbled in delight, yanking on Zed's beard, as if to make sure his attention was focused on her.

"You don't say!" Zed gasped in mock astonishment. "You lit up the whole couch? And then what did silly *papa* do? Did he cry? I bet it was funny when he cried. That's the third couch this year. Did *maman* get pictures?"

The baby seemed to nod and continued her story.

"I know he's just messing with me, that he can't really understand what she's saying," Bael said, staring after them as Zed carried the baby over to the couch so he could tend to Dani. "But the two of them being on the same wavelength? The very idea keeps me awake at night."

Eva pursed her lips. "It should."

EVA HAD ROLLED into town just as the rest of the world seemed to discover Mystic Bayou. She'd never known the Bayou as the small, isolated town it had been. But somehow, it still seemed like a close-knit community, even with the waves of people moving in every week. Eva had never known so many people in one place, not in all of her years living in the human world.

Every time she went to the grocery, she got caught in conversation with someone so long that her ice cream melted. She'd learned to put off frozen stuff until the very end of her shop. She couldn't walk down the street without someone waving and shouting her name. She never sat alone in Rathtilda's Sweet Shoppe. Someone always joined her at her table.

To her surprise, Eva absolutely loved it. Yes, she was useful here. Jon had made it clear that he was losing his business and potentially his luxurious mane of hair before she'd arrived, due to being unable to keep up with demand. But still, her ability to fix damn near anything wasn't the only thing she was valued for in the Bayou. She amounted to more than just her usefulness to others. It meant more than she could possibly let on, for fear of scaring her friends. So she just quietly basked in the daily joys of her life here. Even if they didn't have a single pizza parlor in the whole damn town.

One of the League's initiatives to accommodate the growing population was to put out pop-up "grocery trucks" so people could stop by for basics without flooding the single (Boone-owned) grocery store in town with foot traffic. The League also provided the administrative means for the Boones to open another location at the other end of town – but that was still under construction. And while she normally popped by the truck parked near the Ice Cream Depot if she just needed eggs or milk, this was her "big shop" in the proper grocery store. It wasn't the most scintillating way to spend her Friday night, but well, she was out of chocolate and that could be dangerous for the general population.

Because the Bayou was home to so many cultures, the culinary scope of the shelves was *vast*. Eva could buy anything she wanted from pickled quail eggs to Scotch bonnet peppers. Not that Eva would eat Scotch bonnet peppers, unlike her cousins, who had adored super-spicy foods. She hadn't been able to keep up with them, something they loved to tease her about, but she probably had more of her stomach lining left as a result. Not that she'd spoken to them in the last two hundred years, so she couldn't ask about their digestive health.

Ambling down the aisles, Eva piled Swiss chocolate, pasta, brioche, sesame paste, her preferred stout, and other treats into her cart. And sure, maybe she would get to the eggs and milk, and some vegetables, if she was pressed. The priority, however, was the chocolate.

"Evie!" she heard a tiny voice shout behind her.

She turned to see Bonita De Los Santos pushing her grandson, Tanner, down the candy aisle, careful not to let him within grabbing distance of the gummy worms. Tanner was a daredevil at all of four years old and launched himself out of the cart in a full-body fling. He landed in Eva's arms with absolute confidence that he couldn't be dropped.

Eva might have taken it personally if she hadn't seen him do this to Zed, too. Tanner only seemed to climb the people he saw as "cool." She wrestled him into a cradling position so she could look him in the eye.

"Tanner, buddy, we've talked about warning me first," Eva said, peering down at him. She brushed his shaggy dark hair out of his face.

"But that's no fun," Tanner said, scrunching up his little nose. Eva realized she'd probably just lost cool points in the name of safety, but she was OK with that.

"You get a vote when you pay for your own emergency room visits," Bonita sighed, though she was smirking. "How ya doin', honey? Haven't seen you stop in at your PO Box lately."

"Just busy with work is all," Eva assured her.

"Well, it seems like you've had an uptick in mail lately, so you might want to come clean it out. But if you're grocery shopping on a Friday night, instead of being out on a date, you must be pretty busy," Bonita said.

Eva snorted softly. She wasn't a lawyer, but she knew a leading statement when she heard one. It was the town's worst-kept secret that Bonita was an absolutely incurable gossip. Eva wasn't sure whether that particular trait took hold before or after Bonita's powers as a touch-know psychic developed. Eva suspected that Bonita only took the job as postmaster so she could handle everybody's mail and learn their secrets.

"I normally do my shopping on Sundays, but I needed to check in on Cordelia. She's been feeling a little poorly," Bonita sighed. "I haven't had time to pick up Tanner's favorite snacks. And tonight's movie night, isn't it, sweetheart?"

"We're going to watch the *Fast and the Furious*," Tanner whispered.

Eva looked up at Bonita in alarm, but Bonita nixed the idea with a silent shake of her head. Suddenly, Tanner snagged a package of gummy worms from the shelf and tried to pry it open. Bonita deftly snatched the package out of his hands and chucked it in the cart.

"Cordelia's not feeling well?" Eva asked, frowning.

Cordelia's absence from the festivities at Jon and Lia's made sense now. Like Bonita, Cordelia was a touch-know, a psychic that experienced visions of past events when she held significant objects. She and her boyfriend, Brendan, worked together in artifact storage for the League, supervising the new storage facility outside of town. When Eva had asked after her favorite psychic, Jillian just smiled sadly and said Cordelia had a hard week. For Cordelia, that usually meant handling some sort of ancient weapon that had been involved in something hideous.

"You know she's partial to those biscuit things you make," Bonita noted.

"Rock biscuits!" Tanner cried abruptly. "Are you making rock biscuits, Evie? Can I have some?"

Eva grinned at his eager little face. Her "rock biscuits" were cookies so dense that they ate like a cross between a scone and a chocolate chip cookie. They were a variation on something her grandmother used to make involving nuts and dried fruit. Eva made them when she missed home. Of course, Eva's grandmother hadn't had chocolate all those years ago, so Eva liked to think her version was far superior.

Eva grabbed a bag of semi-sweet chips from the nearby shelf. "I'll make her a batch, check in on her."

"You do that, honey." Bonita winked at her.

"And for me?" Tanner demanded.

"If you're good and let Grandma watch that cartoon about the cows misbehaving on the farm tonight. You know she loves that one," Eva said.

"But there aren't any e'splosions in that one," Tanner said, pouting.

"And yet, I think you'll watch it if I give you *three* rock biscuits," Eva said, eying him carefully. "But you have to eat them one at a time, and maybe share a bite with your grandma."

Tanner sighed, "Fine."

Bonita mouthed "thank you" behind Tanner's back as he blew a raspberry against Eva's cheek, then clamored back into the cart. Bonita wrangled him back down the aisle while Eva headed toward the baking supplies.

As she mentally reviewed the contents of her cabinets at home – baking soda, flour, cinnamon - she noticed the man standing near the end of the aisle. At first glance, there was nothing much unusual about him. He was tall and broad-shouldered, so much so that for a second, she worried that a member of her family had wandered into town. His dark brown hair was lanky and pulled back into a man bun. But he was wearing khakis and a long-sleeved mint green plaid button-down so new she was pretty sure she could see the fold lines from the package. He was peering over his thick, black-framed glasses to study the box in his hands as if he wasn't used to wearing them.

As he continued standing there at the end of the aisle, she realized he was looking at a box of jock-itch medication, and somehow, this collection of contradictions set her teeth on edge. He didn't look like someone considering a penis-related health purchase. He looked like someone *pretending* to be considering a penis-related health purchase. But what was she supposed to do? Alert the management that a man didn't seem sincere in his interest in curative ointment?

Eva turned her cart around, moving in the opposite direction. She walked briskly along the aisles, methodically ticking items off her list. Somehow, her enjoyment of her outing melted away and she just wanted to get through it, go home and bake cookies while watching something from the reality housewives oeuvre. But as she maneuvered through the store, there he was again and again – in the bakery, in the produce, next to the display of discounted canned crawfish. Was he following her? If so, he wasn't being very subtle about it. For goodness' sake, he'd been reading the label on a box of jock-itch treatment like it contained the secrets of the universe.

She frowned, chastising herself for her close-mindedness. Maybe he was shopping for someone at home, someone who was clearly suffering. Maybe he was doing something thoughtful.

His eyes flicked over the rim of his glasses and a shudder ran through Eva's entire body. There was something very wrong with that man's eyes. They were bottomless, so dark they appeared to have no pupils at all. And she swore she could hear screams in her head when she made contact with them.

Nope, nope, nope. Time to go.

She mentally crossed anything frozen off her list of must-haves and steered her cart to the checkout. She could almost feel the man's gaze on her back, like a hot, sweaty, and unwanted hand.

Eva rushed through her transaction and out the door. One of the benefits to being built like she was – being able to carry any damn thing she pleased without struggling. She carried her groceries out to her truck easily, despite two heavy cases of beer and a bottle of bleach. She glanced over her shoulder towards the store, praying she wouldn't see the man.

"You need any help with that?"

Eva was ashamed to say that she nearly jumped out of her skin at the sound of Alex's voice. He was striding across the pavement, looking all windblown and casually handsome, with his shirtsleeves rolled up to his elbow. It was like he'd stepped out of an advertisement for designer cologne, something involving beach backgrounds and long-distance staring. She swallowed heavily, temporarily forgetting the dread behind her in favor of an excited quivering in her belly.

Remembering the anxious dread she'd felt only moments before, Eva glanced over her shoulder. To her surprise, the Man Bun wasn't behind her.

"I thought I should return the favor, since you rescued me the other day," Alex said, grinning at her. It was all she could do not to fan her face in response – good thing her hands were occupied.

"I'm fine, thanks," she said. "But you could grab my keys and open the door."

"Not a problem!"

In that moment, she wished she could suck the words back into her mouth and disappear into the ground. He seemed to scan her body for a moment and then realized she didn't carry a purse. She attached her keys to her belt loops with a carabiner like a sensible person, thank you very much. But that meant he was going to have to put his hands on her waist to unhook the carabiner, and *that* meant there was a strong risk she was going to melt into a puddle of goo on the pavement.

His hands were so gentle as he worked the metal loop loose from her jeans. He didn't grab at her. He didn't treat her like some utility. He carefully unhooked the keys and hit the unlock button on the key fob.

Now that she thought about it, he probably could have just clicked the button without unhooking them. But before she could apologize, he was taking bags out of her hands and loading them into the truck.

"I just wanted to say thank you, again, for your help the other day," he said, grunting a bit as he took the beer case from her hand. "I'd probably still be sitting out in the Devil's Armpit if not for you." He glanced towards her hands, still laden with multiple bags. "How are you carrying all this?"

"Oh, it's nothing," she told him, sidling past him to set the rest of the bags in the truck seat. Up close, he smelled like some smoky, spicy cologne, and her mouth was honest-to-gods watering. Mother of pearl, she should not be allowed out in public.

Alex's head was bent close to hers as he cleared his throat. "I was wondering if–"

He was interrupted by a jovial voice yelling from across the street.

"Hey, Eva! How's it goin' darlin?"

They turned to see Jarvis Luckwell, a newly local boy and a leprechaun, if one could believe it. And while Eva didn't trust him, he was charming in his own way. Well, Jarvis was charming if one could also look past the things that came out of his mouth. It was hard to look past them, but she tried. So, she smiled politely and waved back. "Hi, Jarvis."

"Fancy a drink, then?" he shouted.

She burst out laughing. She wouldn't have a drink with Jarvis Luckwell if that silver flask he was always waving around contained the last known potable water on Earth. But she made it a policy not to antagonize the fae, not in any way or form. "Not right now, Jarvis. I've got perishables to get home. Maybe some other time."

"I'll hold ya to it!" Jarvis crowed, loping down the street like he was mounted on springs.

Eva shook her head and turned back to Alex. "Sorry, what were you saying?"

"Uh, nothing," Alex said, rubbing his hand at the back of his neck. He stepped out of her little bubble of space and backed away. "You have a good night, Eva."

Eva stared after him in confusion as he jogged back to the research village, his shoulders bunched up near his ears. She wondered what she'd done to offend Alex. Still, it was probably better this way. Alex Lancaster was too fine a thing for her to be handling. She'd break him in seconds.

She slammed the truck door shut. She turned to round the bed for the driver's side and a big black truck idled by. The windows were heavily tinted, but the driver's side window rolled down as it passed at a glacial pace. Man Bun stared out the window at her, those dark eyes burning into her skin.

He smirked at her, sending a wave of dread crashing through

her chest. All that confusion over Alex turned to a rage. Who the hell was this guy to be following her around the grocery store and staring at her? Who did he think he was? She was an *Orebender* and she wasn't about to be intimidated by some prick with extremely poor shopping etiquette.

"Move the truck or catch a boot up your ass!" she barked at him.

Man Bun's eyes went wide, all traces of menace in them making way for shock. His tires squealed as his foot apparently landed on the gas. His truck bolted out of the lot like an angry horse. Jessica Galanis, a tiny brunette who worked as Alex's executive assistant, seemed to have caught the whole incident, given the shocked expression on her face.

Eva gave a shrug of her shoulders and climbed into her truck. She was sure that it would be reported back to Alex that she'd been shouting obscenities in public moments after speaking to him. But honestly, if Alex didn't like the fact that she cursed at some guy staring at her, because responding that way wasn't good manners, she could do without him.

"Dickhead," she muttered as she started the truck, though she wasn't sure whom she was referring to.

3

ALEX

TO SAY Alex was unsettled was like saying the Devil's Armpit was a little malodorous.

OK, maybe he was fixated on the Devil's Armpit. It had been days since his little adventure, and he still hadn't gotten the smell out of his hair.

So, yes, Alex was extremely unsettled, not just because he still hadn't found a trucking company to solve the town's distribution issues, but because he had poked his nose in where it probably didn't belong, and he was now confronted with an impossible problem.

He sat back in his ergonomically supportive office chair, prescribed by a League-approved specialist – because that's how many hours he spent in this freaking office. Like almost every space in the research village, it was space gray and non-descript. The chief decoration was a large, framed picture of his parents, black and white, taken while they were on one of their rare family vacations away from the carnival. They were seated on a bench in Gatlinburg, Elliott Carver frowning into the distance while his mother, Gemmie, smiled into the camera held by their son.

"Why take vacations when we're living every else's dream? Don't you know boys your age dream of running away with the carnival?" Elliott used to grumble any time Alex mentioned taking a break. But every few years, seeing her son's desperation to just do *one* normal thing that every other family did, Gemmie would insist on taking a side trip to the mountains or even a big city before they settled into winter in Florida.

Sonja had found the photo loose in one of his moving boxes as he'd unpacked his office. She'd insisted on having it enlarged and framed as a "housewarming" present for him. And then she'd shared some of her precious plants, just to make it "less corporate drone-y." He tried not to take that personally. His was the largest of all the offices in the League's administrative complex, but it was still a far cry from the sleek, mahogany-paneled oasis he'd enjoyed in DC. He'd had acres of space to himself there and a private executive washroom and an espresso machine, all to himself, and a snack bar stocked by a person whose sole job was procuring any obscure and delicious nom the mind could conjure... He really missed the snack bar. But here in the Bayou, he didn't have the other middlemen breathing down his neck, jockeying for a better position. (More specifically, *his* position.) He could focus on the work, on helping people, which wasn't always the focus when he was wading through the politics of League headquarters.

That's what he was trying to do when he decided to meddle. At least, that's what he told himself: he was trying to help. Of course, it was a damn lie, and the internalized fib was catching him right on the ass, just like he deserved.

It had started the other night, when he'd stupidly thought it was some trick of divine providence that he'd ended up at the grocery at the same time as Eva. He hadn't been able to stop thinking about her since she'd rescued him on the side of the road. She was just so *interesting* and compelling and beautiful... and if he was going to be a bit of a bro about it... that ass in those blue jeans... He shook himself. It would not do to have thoughts like that when he was sitting in his office. That could lead to a lot of awkwardness, pants-wise.

Not that any awkwardness had been spared in the parking lot, he supposed. Loading the grocery bags into Eva's truck, Alex was actually in the process of asking her to dinner – the words were literally leaving his mouth – when that local *magie*, Jarvis, had yelled out to her. The leprechaun had asked her out and Eva had just smiled.

In that moment, for the first time in a very long time, Alex lost his nerve. Maybe it was cowardly or superficial, but he just couldn't face the prospect of losing yet another woman he was interested in to yet another local. Especially not a leprechaun. Especially not one named *Jarvis*.

And then he gave himself a very stern lecture about women not being possessions and assured himself that every woman he knew in Mystic Bayou would hand him his own ass, gift-wrapped, if they knew he even had that thought.

Later, Alex told himself that looking Eva up in the League's records could be a way to do something nice for her. He thought maybe he could determine if she qualified for a small business grant for the boat shop or... yeah, he didn't really know what he was looking for, and the justification that he was trying to help her was pretty pathetic. He wasn't even sure she needed help in any way. In fact, it had been a flimsy excuse to look into Eva's background. But now, he was all tangled up in the consequences, and he couldn't in good conscience just sit by and do nothing with the information he had. Or didn't have, for that matter.

Right.

He stood, rolling his shoulders. He took the tie he kept hanging around the knob of his file drawer and slipped it under his collar. He checked the knot in the little mirror he kept under his blotter – because he didn't want to admit he was vain enough to need one or put up with the inevitable teasing if Zed saw it there – and put on what he thought of as his "official face." Professional, impartial, unflappable, definitely not up to his ass in uncertainty. He strode out of his office, shutting the door with a resounding click. His assistant, Jessica, jumped from her seat. "Can I help you, Mr. Lancaster?"

Small, smartly dressed and spiteful, Jessica guarded his door with all the wrath of a pit viper. She'd only recently started speaking civilly to the former office assistant, Leonard, and that was because he'd been moved back to the geology department — now that he was no longer cursed with pathological clumsiness — and not what Jessica considered a threat to her position. Now, if Alex could just get her to speak civilly to everybody else... or anyone else, really.

"Do you know where Sonja is right now?" he asked her as he continued walking to the door. Because if left standing still for too long, Jessica *would* find a way to unleash the inner manticore — metaphorically. She wasn't a shifter, but a descendant of King Midas who could turn anything into gold and yet was also cursed not to profit from it. The fact that Alex had to draw that distinction, even internally, was part of what he loved about working for the League. Nothing was boring.

"Remember when she declared that she and Will would meet every day for lunch at the pie shop? Because *'she and her fiancé deserve to have a personal life, dammit'*?" Jessica said, practically jogging beside him.

"I do remember that. The memory is vivid and somehow, loud," he conceded. "I'm ducking over to the shop. I'll be back soon. Would you like me to pick you up a slice?"

"No, thank you!" Jessica pressing her gloved hand to her chest, looking offended by the very idea that she would eat at her desk. Alex left her there to stew in her professional resentment as he walked across Main Street. It was a more difficult proposition these days, with all the new traffic, but he managed not to get run down like a bad *Frogger* player.

The pie shop was one thing that hadn't changed recently in Mystic Bayou, except maybe that people fought a bit more viciously for seating. The green vinyl booths lined a black-and-white tiled dining room decorated with an odd assortment of kitschy gold-themed art favored by its dragon proprietress. The long counter featured a number of delicious, crusted creations displayed on glass cake stands. Customers stood in line, anxiously eying what was left, glaring at those who had already secured the coveted seats.

Of course, Sonja had managed to get a corner booth four-top, and no one argued with her about taking up that space with only two, because she was Sonja. She and Will sat, talking animatedly over their slices of apple streusel and blueberry lemon. For a second, he stopped in his tracks at the sight of Will's face. Dr. Will Carmody looked like a man who was absolutely contented. He was both at peace and delighted, looking into the eyes of the person he loved more than anything in the known universe. He'd found her and told her how he felt and in return, he'd been given all of the good things life had to offer. And Alex could not have possibly been more jealous of him. Maybe that was why he'd resented Brendan and Jon so much. He was *lonely*.

As rewarding as his work in the Bayou was, he still felt like an outsider here. And he'd never been an outsider, not even when he was traveling with the carnival. He'd been a Carver, with a legendary mender lineage, a lineage he hadn't necessarily wanted to follow himself, but he'd respected it. He'd had a family there, and people surrounding him that felt like family. And then he'd gone on to college and made friends *there*. He changed his name. He'd easily transitioned into working for the League, where he was well-liked by his coworkers, traveling quickly up the ranks until he was one of the most trusted lieutenants, in one of the League's most secretive offices.

And yet, he just couldn't seem to crack the social scene in Mystic Bayou. Sure, Alex might get invited to the occasional board game night by other League employees, but those were polite, empty invitations. His colleagues were afraid to jeopardize their careers by getting too familiar, and the locals didn't trust the League.

Will broke him out of this thought fog by giving Alex a polite-but-not-enthusiastic wave. Alex nodded and navigated the crowded dining room, pretending not to hear the judgmental groans from people in line, wordlessly accusing him of cutting through the wait.

"Alex, I hope there isn't some sort of emergency that merits interrupting my pie time," Sonja said, her expression cordial, but pointed.

"Not exactly, but I wanted to talk to you away from the office in a non-official capacity," Alex said.

Sonja's mien shifted ever so subtly into her professional mode. She nodded sharply and slipped into the other side of the booth with Will. She moved her plate just as Siobhan showed up tableside, plopping a slice of caramel toffee pie in front of him. Siobhan was the cranky brownie artiste who provided all of the shop's pastry. Her magic demanded that she serve customers what she believed they needed to soothe them, to give them strength. Alex had found the lack of menus a little off-putting at first, but now, he was just grateful to have whatever magical support Siobhan could offer.

"You'll know why in a minute," Siobhan commented before toddling off and telling the wait-line customers to "keep your hair on."

Alex had learned not to question Siobhan's cryptic pie commentary. It only slowed down his consumption of said pie.

"So this problem, Alex. Is it a medical crisis?" Will asked quietly.

"It's not another serial killer, is it?" Sonja asked, equally soft.

"Is the rift opening up again?" Will asked.

Sonja hissed, "I knew we shouldn't have trusted that Pandora lady."

"No, no, nothing so dramatic," Alex said, before glancing around to check if anyone local was sitting near their booth. He didn't recognize anyone, so he leaned closer to the table and whispered, "What do you think of Eva Boudreaux?"

Sonja and Will practically melted against each other in relief. All stress and worry evaporated from their faces and they dug into their pie again.

Sonja chewed before pronouncing with her customary authority, "I think she's amazing. Not only has she solved all of Jon's business problems but she's one of the only people who can challenge Jillian at trivia. Of course, it's mostly the earth science questions and physics, but still, she gives the rest of us a fighting chance."

Will shook his head. "No, she doesn't."

"No, she doesn't," Sonja admitted, throwing up her hands. "But I have my pride!"

Will's eyes narrowed, ever so slightly. "Why are you asking about Eva, Alex?"

Suddenly, Sonja's face lit up in glee that if he'd had any sense, probably would have scared the hell out of him. "Oh, wait, are you interested in her?"

Yep, scared right out of him.

He stammered, "O-oh, that's not why I'm asking about her – wait, has she mentioned me?"

"Well, not directly, but she hasn't *not* not mentioned you," she said carefully.

"Was that a triple negative?" Alex asked. Sonja shrugged.

"This whole conversation is starting to feel very junior high," Will muttered into his pie.

What did that mean? That Eva didn't "not not" ask about him? Of all the languages he'd learned over the years, Alex had never quite reached fluency in "female."

"So about Eva–" Somehow, he couldn't quite finish the sentence when he saw Sonja's smile. Yes, she was a coworker, but she was also a person Alex admired, someone he didn't want to upset. And she looked so thrilled when he seemed interested in Eva in any way.

How was he supposed to tell Sonja that her friend wasn't the person she claimed to be? Stalling for time, Alex dug his fork through the crunchy toffee shell to the smooth caramel cream filling – always made from scratch, never from melted store-bought candies. Siobhan would rather swallow a boot. When he chewed through that first bite, he tried to find the right words to share what he'd learned with Sonja. But when he tried to open his mouth, the caramel held his jaw in place. He couldn't talk.

After the initial moment of panic, he snickered, which was hard to do with his teeth stuck together. Somehow, the cantankerous brownie always knew exactly what the customer needed. And while this was a little more directly physical than her usual remedies, she was right. What Alex needed right now was the wisdom to keep his mouth shut.

Alex couldn't tell them what he found, not without talking to Eva first. Not just because it would complicate life for Sonja and Will, but it would hurt Eva. And he was fundamentally opposed to hurting her. It was strange how strongly he felt about it, considering he didn't really know her. But when he thought about causing her trouble, he felt sick down through his feet. Eva was unique, and he'd learned to respect the unique, to give them his due consideration.

Also, talking with his mouth full would have been rude, anyway.

"Yes, what about Eva?" Sonja asked, prompting him.

He pointed to his mouth as he worked through the caramel. He swallowed heavily and finally said, "Um, don't talk to her about me. I'm an adult person. I should probably handle this sort of thing myself."

"Is that really why you came over here," Will asked. "To talk about Eva, but not really?"

"Oh, uh, no, sorry, I just got distracted with the whole Eva thing for a minute," Alex said, then took another bite to give him time to figure out what the hell to say next.

"Is it about the trucking problem?" Sonja asked. "Any solution yet?"

Somehow, it was easier for Alex to chew through this bite as he shook his head. "No, my calls aren't being returned by any of the companies I contacted."

"What is their *deal?*" Sonja asked.

"It's starting to feel organized," Alex admitted. "And a little personal."

"We'll figure something out," Sonja assured him. "I've been thinking about backup plans."

"Some?" Will scoffed, grinning at her. "She has sixteen. Sixteen backup plans."

Alex threw his head back and gave his first honest laugh of the day. "Well, of course, she does."

AFTER WORK, Alex drove out to Eva's house, determined to talk to her about what he'd found, but she wasn't home. And he thought it was probably a little intrusive to wait at her house for her. The last thing he wanted to do was freak her out, so he turned around, heading back to the research village. The late afternoon light cast the town in a sort of golden glow, and for once, the traffic was light, meaning it was quiet and still. It reminded him of the almost idyllic pace the town kept when he'd arrived last year.

He parked his SUV, glancing up the row of tidy Cape Cod-style trailers occupied by the League employees. The coroner, Ivy Portenoy, was leading a round of *Dungeons and Dragons* at a picnic table with a few researchers from the science departments. Cordelia and Brendan were cuddled on the front step of their shared trailer, enjoying a conversation over a Coke. Cordelia never drank, not even in their rebellious youth. It loosened her grip on her psychic gift, which meant terrible nightmares for her.

Alex couldn't help the distant pang of loss he felt in his gut, seeing their heads bent together. Years ago, Alex had loved Cordelia, with all the fierceness of a teenager who believed he was living out *Romeo and Juliet, Carnival Edition*. Cordelia was the talent, using her legitimate psychic powers to cajole the townies into handing over their hard-earned cash. Alex stayed in the background, occasionally working the ticket booths and games between homeschooling sessions. She was funny and smart and tragically beautiful, but even now he didn't know if he'd fallen in love with her *for her*. Somehow, Alex thought he could rescue her from her controlling, manipulative mother. At the time, he'd convinced himself that they were going to run away together for real, make a normal white-picket-fence life somewhere in the suburbs. He had no idea how they thought they would make that happen, but they'd thought they could pull it off. But her mother had other ideas, namely, she didn't want to lose access to her meal ticket. So she'd drugged Cordy's tea, tossed her in their truck and drove her daughter to parts unknown, never to be heard from again.

It was definitely the sort of thing a reasonable parent would do.

Of course, his own father hid the fact that Cordy had written him letters for years afterward. It wasn't until Alex came to Mystic Bayou and they were unexpectedly reunited that they each found out the truth. And sadly, they never got a second chance because she was already smitten with Brendan. It took him some time to accept it, but he'd come around.

While Alex had always thought of Cordy as the one who got away, he knew, ultimately, they wouldn't have worked out long-term. He and Cordy were just dumb kids, craving normalcy like a drug, caught up in the romance and drama of it all. She'd made that clear enough, the one time they hashed through their history. And Alex didn't begrudge Cordelia her happiness. He only wished that he could find some of his own.

A reminder alarm sounded on his phone and he sighed, bumping his head back on the driver's seat. Speak of the devil. Alex always called his parents on Tuesday nights, as long as there wasn't some crisis brewing. Midweek nights were generally pretty light for his parents, work-wise – which was a strange thought to have when your parents were in their late sixties.

Alex didn't know if his parents would ever retire. Driving around the country was getting harder and harder on them both. And his father was getting older, though Elliott didn't want to admit it. But Elliott Carver just didn't have it in him to be still, to not be of any use. It was like Elliott thought that if he stopped working, he would die. That was what Alex told himself when his father didn't come to the phone. Elliott was too busy preventing his own death.

Still, Alex dutifully dialed the number, knowing his mother would answer on the first ring. "Hi, Mom."

"Sweetheart!" she exclaimed. He knew exactly where Gemmie was, standing in their trailer, fixing his father a home-cooked dinner better than he could find in the communal cook tent. Gemmie had a talent for bookkeeping, so she generally served as the unofficial accountant for whatever operation they worked for – as long as the owners would turn the ledgers loose. But any hours that weren't filled with her special approach to creative math were occupied with keeping their family trailer the coziest of any home in the caravan – classical music, clean clothes, wholesome meals. It was the best she could do to fill Alex's hunger for that bit of "normal" during his childhood.

"How are you!" she asked as if they hadn't spoken for years instead of just a few days before. He could hear the off-key metallic plinking of the carousel music in the background, filtering through the walls of the trailer as if it was coming from underwater. His chest ached with homesickness, just for a moment. Even if he didn't miss everything about how he grew up, there were bits that struck a chord. "How's work?"

"Same old, same old," he said.

"Well, with your job, that could mean anything," she snorted.

"That's true," he admitted. "But same goes to you and Dad."

His mother charged on, "You have no idea what it's like, having a son who's very important and involved in things on the news that everybody is talking about and not being able to say anything to *anybody* about it. Connie Sage brags about her son, Derek, getting a job with some web site that ranks food trucks by zip code, like that's some big accomplishment. My son works for the *League*, runs his whole department, a whole town, and I have to pretend like you have some boring office job going nowhere."

Alex barely withheld his snicker. Connie Sage's husband was

master of the old "weight guessing" game, but she'd been a thorn in Gemmie's side for years, talking anyone's ear off about her perfectly average son like he was personally responsible for finding a cure for chicken pox and texting thumb. "Well, people love food trucks."

"Food trucks move around a lot," she noted. "Sort of makes ranking them by zip code a pointless proposition."

He grinned, his shoulders shaking with silent laughter. "Well, you know why you can't tell anybody about me, Mom. It wouldn't be safe for either of us."

"I know," she grumbled. "But if Connie only knew…"

"Maybe it would take your mind off of Connie if you two came and visited me sometime," he said carefully. "I know your busy season is coming up, but I'm in one place, so I'm easy to find."

His mother sighed.

"We'll try, sweetheart, but I can't make any promises. You know how your father is. He thinks the world will just fall apart without him, so he never takes time off," Gemmie said.

Despite himself, Alex rolled his eyes. It wasn't like his dad was appealing death penalty cases. He was keeping a carnival afloat. The way of life Alex had grown up with was changing, thanks to the over-crowding of the average family's calendar. People just didn't go out for a night at the carnival as much as they used to, and while that was sad, Elliott seemed to resent it more and more every year. And he seemed to resent Alex for leaving the carnival, when he'd been the one who encouraged Alex to go out into the world, to go to law school and make a life away from it.

Any other parent would be *proud* of how Alex had turned out. Gemmie was proud, so proud that it annoyed her that she had to keep quiet about his accomplishments. But Elliott?

Aloof, that was the only word for it. Alex had done exactly what Elliott had hoped for him, but now he held himself apart. And every year, the chasm between them grew wider and wider. His poor mother was the only one who tried to bridge it, and Alex felt terrible doing that to her. It had to be *exhausting*.

"It's been three years, Mom. And I came to see you. At a camp-ground. In Arkansas. In July."

"I know, I know," she sighed. "I'll talk to him. But let's, you and me, talk about something else. How's that bear fella? And your friend whose baby keeps burping fire?"

Alex rubbed the back of his neck. He never revealed anyone's name or position with the League or the town, but his mother found the various magical gifts of his colleagues to be fascinating. And urges to brag to Connie Sage aside, his mother's discretion could be trusted.

And so, he gave her anonymous updates about his coworkers and acquaintances, not correcting her assumption that they were his friends. She imagined her son as a popular man who was beloved by the town that he ran (single-handedly, obviously). He didn't have the heart to tell her he didn't have friends here, that he was tolerated because he kept things running (mostly) smooth. He didn't see the harm in it, unless, of course, she finally took him up on the offer to come visit. But knowing his father, that would never happen.

After a lengthy discussion of his "mermaid friend" who fixed boats, Alex said goodnight to his mother and climbed out of the car. He chose not to look towards Cordelia and Brendan's trailer because he didn't want to come across like a sad creep staring at the happy couple. So instead, he kept his eyes trained toward the town square, where he happened to see Eva, sitting at the gazebo.

Shit.

Reality intruded into the little bubble of mental peace he'd built with his conversation with his mother. He really shouldn't put off this conversation. Taking a deep breath, he put that unflap-pable professional mask on and jogged across the street. The gazebo was a bandshell with a large swing suspended from the ceil-ing. While it used to be simple to sit on that swing and contem-plate the town and all its mysteries, now Eva shared it with a handful of tourists, who were snapping pictures of the parish hall.

She was sitting on the swing, poking a plastic picnic fork into a to-go container from the pie shop.

She looked... radiant. All of the light of the setting sun seemed to absorb into her hair, making it glow in all manner of metallic shades, and somehow, her skin glowed, too. She was wearing those sunglasses that hid her eyes from him, but she seemed content, sitting there, staring into the growing twilight.

And he was about to mess all that contentment up.

He cleared his throat and when she looked up at him and smiled, his heart stuttered like he'd been electrocuted. Turn around, he told himself, turn around so you don't take that smile away. But then he remembered what he'd found and pressed forward.

"Hi Alex!" she called with a brightness that made his chest tight and hot all at once. "I'm just enjoying a little 'end of the day' pie, which was completely different from my 'beginning of the day' pie and my 'middle of the day' pie."

"I need to talk to you," Alex said quietly

"Is everything all right?" she asked, frowning and putting her pie aside.

The others were too close, he realized. He didn't want the tourists to overhear what he was about to say. He didn't want to embarrass her, make a scene. So as gently as he could, he took her pie from her hands and set it aside, pulling her to her feet. He was trying to figure out how he was going to urge her out of the gazebo when she jerked her hands out of his. He immediately felt the loss, not touching her anymore, but filed that feeling away for later when he could wrestle with it.

"Do you know what happens to people when they get between me and a slice of banana cream pie?" she demanded, her brow furrowed. "I'm trying to recreate the recipe at home, and I can only get Siobhan to 'prescribe' it to me every once in a while. I have to *pretend* to have work stress to get it! Do you *know* how hard it is to fool her?"

It was the least pleasant expression he'd seen on her face since they'd met, and it filled him with a mix of dread and certainty. Before, he'd sensed that he was building something with her and what he was about to say would smash that foundation into nothing. She snatched her pie off of the swing but still followed him as he gestured toward the fountain.

He watched as she deliberately tried to school her features into less angry lines. And she failed because he was obviously pissing her off pretty successfully. Through gritted teeth, she asked, "Alex, what is going on? I don't know you very well, but this seems like, um, not the norm for you."

Right. If he was going to do this, no sense in trying to dance around it. He swallowed heavily before asking, "What's your real name?"

Her mouth, her beautiful, lush mouth, fell open in shock, and he was instantly sorry. He wanted to pull the words back into his own lips, to take away that distress painted across her face. He wanted to yell "Just kidding!" and run away. But he'd already started down this road and there was no stopping now.

"Is that how people start conversations where you're from?" she asked, her brow so deliberately furrowed, he knew her confusion couldn't be genuine.

"Your real name. I don't want to embarrass you. I'm sorry, Eva, but your personal history doesn't add up."

"And what are you doing looking in the first place? My 'personal history' is none of your business." Her lips drew back from her even white teeth. He was reminded that while he didn't know what sort of *magie* Eva was, she was clearly some sort of otherworldly creature. He suspected that she had the strength to rip off his face if she wanted, and somehow, that didn't make her less beautiful in his eyes, only more fascinating.

There was something very wrong with him, to be having these thoughts right now in the middle of this conversation.

"Well, I make it my business to take an interest in anyone who spends time with the League's core leadership. You haven't been here very long, Eva, and yet, you've made a place for yourself, right in the inner circle. League leaders, town leaders, you're right in the midst of them. And I'm sure you have your reasons for living here under a false identity, but those things combined make me very nervous, considering everything that's happened in the bayou over the last few years."

"None of what you just said makes sense," she said, shaking her head. "I'm not living under a fake name. I'm not here to hurt anyone and fuck you for thinking that I would."

A sharp pinching dart of pain hit Alex right in the sternum at her words, but he ignored it as Eva added, "You must have made a mistake when you were rooting around in my business, which – just one more time, to emphasize my point – *you had no business doing.*"

"There were no Eva Boudreauxs born on your birthdate in any place in the United States, which is where your documents were supposedly issued," he told her flatly. "Whoever you paid to put her life together for you did an admirable job, but the holes are there for someone who knows how to look."

Unease flickered across her expression, but she got it back under control in seconds. She shrugged lightly. "Boudreaux could be my married name."

"There were no Eva Boudreauxs with your birthdate married in the last century in any place in the United States," he said.

"I could have legally changed my name because I happen to like the name 'Boudreaux,'" she countered, and there was a strange hint of a smile around her lips like she was enjoying this somehow. He didn't know if that gave him hope or scared the hell out of him, maybe both. Probably both.

He pursed his lips, and for a moment, he thought about dropping the whole thing. "Nope, I ran that check, too."

She scoffed. "How?"

"I work for the League? Unlimited and slightly less than legal resources are a side benefit of the job. Your documents, while very good, are fake. I couldn't find any real record of who you are, where you're from or what you did before you came here. And considering those resources I mentioned, that's both impressive and distressing. I was able to at least confirm that someone with your photo on her driver's license attended multiple mechanical programs under the Eva Boudreaux identity, so at least you're not lying to Jon about your qualifications."

For the first time, Eva looked really, truly angry and Alex decided he was definitely more scared than hopeful.

"My name *is* Eva, and my qualifications are real, thank you very much," Eva said. "As for my real last name and birthdate and everything else, I don't have to give it to you, because it's none of your business. Who the hell do you think you are?"

"The League executive director," Alex answered. "Your neighbor. A friend, I hoped. I'm just trying to protect the people here, the people who are important to me, the people who are important to what we do here in Mystic Bayou. And if you're a threat to that, Eva, I can't have you here, no matter how much I like you."

Alex felt like he was very quickly becoming an expert interpreter of Eva Whatever-Her-Last-Name-Was's ever-shifting facial expressions. But even he had difficulty separating the shock that his words put there, followed by denial and even a bit more anger. Why would she be angry that he said he liked her? Was he really so awful that it was bad news? OK, maybe he was wrong when he assumed they'd been building a connection, but he thought they could at least be civil to each other.

"You *like me?*" she seethed, her face a breath away from his. "Well, you have a funny way of showing it."

He had the destructive, insane urge to press his lips to hers, to try to stop all that anger from coming out of her mouth, to show her that his affection was real, even if it was new. But again, she could probably tear his face off, and he needed his face. It was attached to a lot of stuff.

Fortunately, Eva turned away from him, shoulders set in a rigid line. She didn't *stomp* across the street, but it was pretty close before she whirled around and came right back to growl, "And again, just because I feel like you need to hear this — *really hear it,* dammit – I would never do anything to put anyone here in danger. They're my family, too."

Before he could stop himself, he shot back. "They're not *my* family. I don't have a family, not like that anyway."

She inhaled sharply and the angry tension in her mouth softened. "Well, that's the saddest fucking thing I've ever heard."

"I know you're angry with me, Eva, but I need answers."

"Well, you're not going to get them. You don't deserve them." She turned again towards her truck and took a few steps but changed her mind and returned to him. In a much calmer tone, she said, "I have my reasons for how my records look, all right? I promise you, I won't hurt anyone. I would appreciate if you would keep what you found to yourself until *I* decide what I'm going to tell the others. You dug into my life without any provocation. It's not my fault that you didn't like what you found. I didn't do anything to deserve it. You owe me, not the other way around."

In that moment, Alex made a decision. He'd met his professional obligations by confronting Eva with what he found. Technically, he didn't have to ask her to leave town or call the League's more authoritative branches because he hadn't found anything incriminating in Eva's records. It was just the lack of information that was disturbing. For all he knew, Eva was the victim of some crime, which honestly, he should have thought of before he talked to her. He was so worried about defending the town, he didn't consider that Eva might need defending.

He was an idiot.

"All right," he said, nodding. "But when you're ready, and it needs to be soon, we need to talk again."

"Fine."

He watched her walk towards her truck without another word, stopping to toss her pie into the garbage. She climbed in and slammed the door behind her. She didn't move for several minutes, her head bent over the steering wheel as she breathed deeply.

However badly he thought it was going to be, he'd made it so much worse. His brain screamed at him to cross the road, tell her he was sorry, that she'd taken away his ability to think and reason and not behave like a complete asshole. But he didn't think she wanted to hear his excuses. She just wanted him to leave her alone.

Eva pulled carefully out of her parking spot, steering towards Sea Cove Road. He watched her drive off into the purpling dark, regret aching in his gut. A black pick-up truck with heavily tinted windows trundled quietly behind her down the street.

Alex frowned. It looked like the same truck that had been following her the other night, but he couldn't be sure it was the same one or even that it was following Eva. And again, he doubted Eva wanted to hear from him.

"Idiot," he sighed.

THE WORLD just made more sense with engine parts in Eva's hands, and not much about the last day or so made sense.

It was Jon's turn to pick music today, so the Rolling Stones echoed through the spotless, well-organized workshop at Carmody and Boudreaux, wailing about their lack of satisfaction. Jon had a thing about classic rock, while Eva was more of a "I know what I like" type. It came in handy when, on her days, Eva occasionally picked dubstep-remixed sea shanties just to mess with Jon.

Some of them were pretty catchy.

Staring into the engine of a fishing trawler suspended over her workstation with chains for easy access, Eva wondered how Alex had picked her façade apart so easily? And why had he bothered to look in the first place? It was frightening, to imagine why he was digging around in her background, even though she'd barely talked to the man.

He didn't have to say he liked her, she thought, turning a wrench over in her hands. That singed her feelings, and she wasn't supposed to be flammable. Standing there on the street, she couldn't help the feeling of rage that had coursed through her when he said he "liked" her. What was he playing at, saying that to her? Men like Alex Lancaster didn't *like* her, not that like that, at least.

They liked talking engines with her or they tried to mull over their lady problems with her because she was "so easy to talk to." She was comfortable in the friend zone with men that felt untouchable - so why would he bother saying it? Did he want something from her? Maybe he was only pretending that he couldn't find her real identity, what with those bottomless League resources he was going on about? Maybe it was all some ruse to get to…

Never mind that.

Eva wasn't even sure why she'd gotten so mad at him over it. Maybe it was because she'd taken one look at Alex, and even after he'd revealed his annoyingly likeable personality during their encounter on the side of the road, she'd put him in – well, not even the "friend zone." She'd put him in the "meh zone," as in, "Yeah, he's really handsome and has a good sense of humor and doesn't take himself too seriously, but 'meh,' I just don't think it's going to go anywhere beyond a passing acquaintance." And then he came along and pretended to be interested in her? That just seemed *mean*.

She couldn't imagine what had prompted it, other than maybe the League knew about the sapphire? There were all sorts of legends about the stone's supposed power, not that she'd experienced anything in her time with it. But if League administration thought she had it, would they send Alex to try to charm its whereabouts out of her? Somehow, that was simultaneously insulting and hurtful.

For a moment, it made her want to run, to pack all her stuff in her trailer and move on to some other town, maybe somewhere north and cold, a complete change of picture. And then she remembered the roots she'd laid down in this town, the fact that she *owned* something here, ran a business. So, she tamped down that urge and stayed put. But that didn't help her desire to avoid Alex all together, despite his impertinent fucking demands that she eventually explain herself to him. What gave him the right? Well, OK, the powerful, worldwide shadow government he worked for gave him the right, she supposed. But still, it was a little aggressive.

She didn't want to go anywhere near him, much less talk to him – and here she was, heading over to Cordelia's that evening after work to check in on her, because she'd promised Bonita she would. It was unfortunate that Cordelia lived a few doors down from Alex in pretty tight quarters, but there wasn't much she could do about it. She'd given her word, and Cordelia was a friend. So was Bonita, for that matter.

"So, I was thinking," Jon said.

"*GAH!*" Eva exclaimed.

Jon was supposed to be at the computer, printing invoices, because it was his turn for that much-hated chore. Instead, he was at her side, speaking in her ear, startling her so badly that she flailed, knocking the chain holding the engine up off its hook. The engine, which was not-exactly-light and definitely-not-cheap, tumbled out of its loops and dropped toward the concrete floor. Eva crouched, catching its bulk awkwardly against her chest, but steady enough to lower it to the floor.

Jon was staring at her, his mouth hanging open.

She shrugged. "What?"

"You know that was a couple hundred pounds of iron you just caught like it was a medicine ball, right?" Jon asked.

"There's some plastic in there, too. But yeah." She nodded.

"I mean, I knew you were strong, but I didn't know you were *that* strong. I'm not sure even Zed could have pulled that off," Jon marveled. "But please don't tell him I said that because he'll see it as a challenge and destroy everything in this building trying to do it. Also, he would probably challenge you to an arm-wrestling contest."

"Noted. Do not give Zed inspiration for expensive feats of strength," Eva said.

Jon pressed his lips together, squinting at her. "OK, I'm just going to choose not to ask more questions and assume you will one day explain your superhero origin story after the evil genius chasing you drives a giant robot through the town."

"It's not quite that dramatic," she assured him. This was probably the moment to do what she'd promised Alex, to explain herself to her friends before she confessed all to him. But she just didn't have it in her right now. She didn't want her story to come spilling out to Jon because she caught an engine like a medicine ball. "So, why did you sneak up on me?"

"Yeah, that was probably a bad idea, come to think of it. So, uh, I was over in Golden Acres at the parts store, and I ran into an old friend. He's a tow truck driver, originally from over in Galveston. Nice guy. A kelpie, but I don't hold that against him. Even if most of his family are enormous pains in the ass." Jon scratched the back of his neck and for a moment, looked extremely uncomfortable. "He's single."

Eva's head dropped. "Oh, come on, Jon."

"I just thought he might be your type!" Jon said as she wiped her hands on her bandana. It was lime green today and printed with dancing Sasquatches, a gift that Jillian found on some obscure web site. "And you haven't dated anyone since you got into town."

"That you've seen," she said, smirking at him. "As a matter of fact, I've enjoyed the company of several gentlemen since I moved here. OK, two. I've enjoyed the company of two gentlemen since I moved here."

Jon's brows drew up. "Really? Anybody I know?"

"Nope," she said, grinning at him. "Are we really talking about this?"

Jon threw his arms up. "I've heard that this is what friends talk about! Well, I heard it from Zed and Will, so who knows if it's true. But when all of the guys are together, all I hear is 'Jillian this, and Dani that.' And of course, Will talks about Sonja all the damn time, but who can blame him? I can't talk with you about Lia because you see her all the time and I think I would just be telling you stuff you already know about how amazing *she* is. Ergo–"

"Ergo?" she snorted. "You *have* been spending too much time with Sonja."

"False. There is no such thing as too much time with Sonja," he shot back, sounding downright prim. "*Ergo*, I have to ask you about people you're interested in, because you don't ever talk about it. That's the one thing we never seem to talk about. I don't even know if you've ever been in a relationship."

"Did you like talking about relationships when you *weren't* in a relationship?" she asked.

He chewed that over for a moment, leaning against the stainless-steel worktable. "That is a very good point. Look, you're one of my favorite people, Eva. And I don't like a lot of people."

"The list seems to be expanding every day," she noted.

"The group doesn't count. They're family, like you," he said. "I just want you to be happy. And I'm not saying it's impossible to be happy when you're single, so don't go beating me on the head with that. I'm not an asshole. But I see how you look at everybody else when we're all spending time together. You seem to want some of it for yourself. And *if* you want that, I want to help you find it."

"Well, I don't think you're gonna find it for me at the marine parts store."

Jon shrugged. "You never know."

"I'm not actively looking for what y'all have, but I'm also not gonna turn it away if I find it," Eva said. "But I don't want you going out searching for someone for me, like it's some scavenger hunt. One thing I've learned is the harder you look for something like that, the less likely you are to find it. If I'm supposed to find someone, they'll show up in my life. Look at you and Lia. You weren't looking for her and she just jumped into your backyard naked."

"Yeah, that doesn't seem like something that happens to a lot of people, though," he said.

"Probably not." She paused and checked her watch, deciding she wasn't going to make any progress until she got the engine back on the chains, and she didn't have the energy to do that until the morning. "I think I'm gonna head over to Cordy's. Bonita says she's not feeling great. I'm taking her some rock biscuits."

"Aw, that's nice of you." He gave her what she assumed was an impersonation of Zed's "baby Dalinda eyes." She sighed. "I left some for you and Lia on the kitchen table."

"And, besides your superpowers, that is why you're my best friend," Jon said.

"Weirdo."

———

EVA KNOCKED on the door of Brendan and Cordelia's trailer. Brendan answered the door, his face even paler than usual. Brendan was a rare male banshee, meaning he occasionally, without any forewarning, predicted the deaths of people in his immediate vicinity by screaming. And sometimes, throwing up. It always made Eva a little nervous to spend time around him, because she didn't like the idea of knowing when she was going to die. But she tried not to let her distress show as he was just so *nice*. And he made Cordelia happy, which counted for a lot in her book.

"Ah! Eva, kind of you to stop by," he exclaimed, his lilting Irish accent not nearly as grating to her ears as Jarvis Luckwell's. He nodded to the Tupperware container with her rock biscuits. "And you baked, so even more friendship points to ya!"

"How's the patient?" Eva asked quietly. "Bonita said she hasn't been well."

Brendan's smile was thin as he closed the door a bit. "We got too comfortable, that's all. My Cordelia has handled everything the League has sent us so far so easily, she let her guard down. Last week, they sent us a real nasty piece of business. That's all I can say."

He glared over her shoulder, toward Alex's place. It was all Eva could do not to turn and do the same. It was at times like this, Eva was grateful that her gifts were of a more mundane, earth-bound nature. Yes, she worked long hours on her feet, but at least she wasn't haunted by nightmares of engine parts and motor oil.

"Frankly, I wonder if the League sent her some dangerous article on purpose," Brendan added, "Just to remind us that they're still in charge. Sonja is looking into it. But Cordelia's a tough one. I'm trying to get her to eat and rest long enough to recover, but she won't sit still! She's gonna need time and rest to build herself up again."

"I'll see if I can help with that," Eva said, raising the Tupperware. "I will stuff her full of carbs until she submits."

"I'd be ever so grateful if you did." Brendan blew out a relieved breath. "Cordelia, love, Eva's come to visit you!"

He opened the door wider to reveal Cordelia stretched on their couch, one of Clarissa's crazy quilts tucked around her. She and Brendan had used little touches like that to personalize their living space – framed photos of themselves, photos of their friends, a little porcelain cottage that must have looked something like Brendan's home in Ireland, given its pride of place.

Like the banshee, Cordelia was looking pretty pasty, with deep purple circles under her eyes. After months of knowing her, Eva was aware that Cordelia's gift took a lot out of her, but still, Eva had never seen her looking so frail. Somewhere, in Eva's gut, anger flared hot and bright. She wasn't even sure who she was angry at – Cordy for not taking care of herself, the League for putting Cordy in the position where she was so worn out. Eva knew it was a pointless reaction, but it didn't stop her from feeling it. She had a soft spot for the psychic, who had helped Eva ease gently into Jon's circle of friends. Jon was happy to include her in all of his invitations, but he was still getting used to spending time around people after years of self-imposed seclusion.

Like Eva, Cordy wasn't quite accustomed to large gatherings or female friendships, so they helped each other figure them out. When they were overwhelmed by the noise and crowds at the parties, they sort of huddled together off to the sides, chatting quietly. And the others were kind enough not to point it out.

Cordelia smiled wanly up at Eva from her cozy little nest. "Come on in!"

Cordy tried to shift up to her elbows, but Brendan rushed across the room to help her. "Easy there, darlin, you're not quite up to fighting form, yet."

"I'm fine," Cordy insisted, even as she sagged back against the cushions. "I've been on this couch for days. Eventually, you're going to have to let me have crazy adventures like sitting up on my own."

"Keep up the sass and I'll tell Eva all about your 'adventure' attempting to make breakfast this morning," Brendan told her, moving to the kitchen, where a kettle started shrieking on the stove. "Eva, did you know eggs can explode when they boil dry, because someone left them on the stove while they passed out on the couch?"

"I did not know that very specific fact about eggs," Eva said, shaking her head.

"He's being dramatic," Cordelia insisted. "It was just a *small* fire."

Brendan stepped out of the kitchen with two steaming mugs in his hands. He handed one to Cordelia and another to Eva. It was good old-fashioned Earl Grey, with a dollop of honey, just the way she liked it. She winked at Brendan.

"Well, if you're really not doing that poorly, I guess you don't need these," Eva said, showing her the rock biscuits.

"The chocolate chip ones!" Cordelia gasped. "I am doing *very* poorly. I am barely hanging on. I am practically at death's door. And the only thing that will cure me is about six of those."

"I heard that," Brendan called, having returned to the kitchen. "You just admitted to infirmity. Eva, you're a witness."

Eva said, "I won't sign anything, for the sake our friendship."

Cordelia preened, so Eva added. "But you're going to keep your ass on that couch, or I'll figure out a way to weld you to it."

Cordelia responded with an epic pout. Brendan snickered,

leaning in to kiss Cordelia. "I'll just pop over to the shop for the makings for dinner. I leave her under your supervision, Eva."

"That's insulting!" Cordelia noted. "I'm a grown woman."

"There's egg yolk on the ceiling, darlin," he reminded her, pointing to a round yellow splotch on the plastic overhead. "An entire singed egg yolk. Intact. On our ceiling."

"Fine," Cordy sighed.

Brendan winked at Eva as he headed for the door. "If you can get her to drink more than one tea, you'll be my hero."

"Hydration is the name of the game," Eva said, with a little salute.

"Good girl, yourself," Brendan said.

"So, what did you do?" Eva asked after Brendan left.

"Well, I can't tell you what it was, only that it's safely contained and a real mean sonofabitch," Cordelia heaved an enormous breath, pretending it was to cool her tea. "I just put a hand on the shipping crate and the next thing I know, I'm lying on my back in the warehouse and Brendan is hovering over me *completely* freaking out. He wanted to call an ambulance, but I reminded him that one, we really don't have those here and two, that's a huge violation of League protocol. And while he argued with me on the topic of 'League Protocol and Whether It Can Go Straight to Hell,' he called Zed out to the site to help haul me into the clinic. Zed used his full powers of adoptive brother guilt. It was completely unfair."

"That is dirty pool, Brendan," Eva told him.

"All's fair in love and keeping your most cherished person conscious," he retorted, closing the door behind him.

"I will think about that when my brain is fully functional," Cordy replied, biting into a rock biscuit. She chewed, a blissful expression on her face. "I'm sorry I missed the game night."

"Jillian played against all of us. Her gloating was downright demoralizing."

"That sounds about right." Cordy laughed before sinking back against the cushions. "I just feel so stupid. You would never let something like this happen to you."

"You ever had an engine block for a fishing trawler dropped on you? Because that stings."

Cordelia cackled. "No, but I haven't led the strange and colorful life you have."

"Um, you grew up in a carnival."

Cordelia was still laughing when Eva cleared her throat. "I had a bit of an argument with Alex the other night."

Cordelia's mouth fell open. "Really? In general, Alex isn't a confrontational person."

"He looked into my records, found holes in my story," Eva said. "Told me I needed to explain myself to him. He didn't give me a deadline or anything, but the 'or else and soon' was implied."

"Well, that's no good," Cordelia said, chewing thoughtfully.

Cordelia knew that her name wasn't Eva Boudreaux and that she wasn't from Louisiana. But that's about all Eva had shared with her, as tight as they were. Eva hadn't even told Jon yet, and since they'd become the closest of friends, Eva felt she owed it to him to tell him first. She just hadn't worked up the nerve yet. She wasn't entirely sure she was ever going to say anything, and then Alex came crashing along and made a mess of everything.

"I'm more disappointed than worried," Eva sighed. "I mean, I could tell Alex was sort of tightly wound when it came to work stuff, but I thought he was, I don't know, nicer than this?

Then again, I've only had a few conversations with him and the two of you grew up together. How worried should I be?"

"Well, like I said, Alex isn't confrontational, or some asshole who just goes around trying to mess up people's lives. For him to have said anything to you, he must be pretty concerned. It might be better for you to just tell him what he wants to know to put his mind at ease. I know you don't want to, and you shouldn't have to, but it might make things easier for you in the long run."

"Or he could mind his own damn business and leave me alone," Eva suggested.

"He could, but it's sort of his job to protect the community from threats," Cordy explained gently. "And it's not like we haven't had threatening situations, several of them, just since Alex took over."

"I wish you wouldn't make rational points for him in such a reasonable and sensible manner," Eva grumbled into her tea.

Cordy smiled gently, giving Eva knowing look. "So, are you angry with him because he looked into your past? Or because you felt secure before and now you don't?"

"Both," Eva muttered.

"Well, you can't run forever. That's what I've learned anyway. And Alex is a good man," Cordy told her. "Not my kind of man, obviously, but a good man. And personally, I find it interesting that he looked into your records without any real reason. Alex is busy enough that he wouldn't just do that unless he had some sort of special interest."

"Yeah, if nosiness and blackmail are considered special interests," Eva said.

"You know that's not what I meant," Cordelia replied.

"I know what you meant, but I'm ignoring it because we're talking about reality, not science fiction."

Cordelia threw up her hands. "I'm just saying, stranger couples have happened here in the bayou."

"Name one," Eva countered.

"Do you really want to talk about the Beasleys and their dating lives?" Cordelia asked.

"No, no, I do not." Eva shuddered. "Sorry to bring this to your door when you're already run-down."

Cordy scoffed. "Are you kidding? I'm glad to focus on someone else's problems for a bit. Keeps my mind off exploding eggs."

———

EVA DECIDED to take the first step in resolving this whole mess, telling Jon, on her own terms, and not when she'd only just dodged an engine falling on her. She parked her truck outside Jon's house. He was at home, with Lia. She could see them on the couch through the window, all curved around each other like puzzle pieces.

As she approached the door, crossing the little wooden bridge that led to the porch, Eva smelled something strange on the wind, like rotten eggs. Frankly, it smelled a lot like the Devil's Armpit. Eva supposed it could have been some foul methane drifting over from the swamp, but Jon's house always smelled like the fresh wind off the ocean. It was one of the benefits of his nature. Somehow, breathing in this smell made her teeth grind. She felt a prickle of fear sweeping down along her arms. She was being watched. Not just observed, but *watched.*

Or maybe her body was just reacting to how much she was dreading this conversation.

Before she could even knock on the door, Jon opened it, his brows drawn together. To her surprise, she actually felt tears welling up in her eyes at the sight of his face. She was going to have to explain so many lies, and Jon was going to *hurt.* Her best friend in the world was about to find out what an absolute liar she was.

"You OK, Evie?" he asked, reaching out for her.

"I've got some things to tell you," she said, sighing. "You're going to want to get some of that terrible beer."

5

___

ALEX

JILLIAN RAMSAY, Ph-Damn-D, was a woman who had found her place in the world.

Seriously, it said, "Ph-Damn-D" right there on her little desk plaque. Alex was pretty sure Zed had made it for her.

Alex sat in Jillian's office, surrounded by pictures of Jillian's baby and Bael, which seemed to occupy all of the places that weren't already taken up by pictures of her little family she'd built. And while envy of this position was nothing new for him, it had taken on an even sharper edge this morning, when he got notice that Cordelia and Brendan were moving out of their League housing. They'd secured a tract of land, some corner of Zed's family property that he insisted Cordy was entitled to as his informally adopted sibling, and they were going to build a house on it. (Who knew what they were going to use for building materials, but that wasn't his problem.)

It was the third notice like it he'd received that week, and he was starting to wonder if he was going to be the only one left of the League employees that originally moved into the village. He still had a town to run, and it was going to be a lot more difficult if he couldn't just shout out the window at his nearest neighbor to ask them a question. Not that he did that very often, but when he did, it was a very useful administrative shortcut.

Also, did Jillian's baby have a fang sticking out of her mouth in that photo? Before he could lean closer to get a better look at the photo on the desk, Sonja and Jillian walked in carrying binders and files, moving briskly as they always did. Sonja wore a silk blouse the color of spring violets, that was somehow spotless and perfectly pressed despite the heat. Jillian had a nickel-sized hole burned in the shoulder of her cobalt sweater – he assumed the casualty of some sort of spit-up incident with her daughter – but still exuded the picture of professional calm. He instantly felt better for their being there, less alone. He didn't have to handle all of this mess by himself.

"Morning!" Sonja called. "Big agenda today, so we better get started."

Alex cleared his throat and put on that professional mask. They spent the better part of two hours going over all of the logistical issues that popped up when a town's population increased exponentially in such a short amount of time. It wasn't just housing and goods. There were infrastructure issues, plus problems with the roads and sewers and power grids. They were in the process of building a proper hospital because the clinic couldn't keep up with the demand. As community liaison, it was Jillian's job to make sure the interests of the locals were being represented. And Sonja's job was to make it happen as smoothly as possible, even while it challenged her considerable skills. Alex tried to see all these problems as a sign of hope, of progress being made, but most of it was a giant pain in his ass.

Sonja closed her PowerPoint presentation on construction of the new tourism center.

"So, to sum up, even more people are coming into town. We are completely overrun and we have more problems than ever before. But other than that, everything is fine."

"Oh, good, I was afraid you were going to wrap up on a gloomy note," Jillian snorted.

"It's not all bad news," Sonja said. "It's just going to be a lot of work and we need more of everything, more people, more supplies, more housing, more places to put the supplies. The irony being that we can't build those places unless we get more supplies."

"Sometimes I wonder whether we would have been better off if Mystic Bayou was still a secret," Jillian sighed. "Which it would be if I'd never written that book."

"If you hadn't, you never would have met Bael or had the baby," Sonja reminded her.

"OK, good point," Jillian conceded. "But I could have made the place sound far less charming."

"Yes, how dare you make a dry, bureaucratic report bearable – nay, entertaining to read," Alex retorted. "Look, I know this has been a bit of a nightmare trying to hold everybody together, to make room, but it's not like we can turn people away or put the genie back in the bottle. People know we're here now. And if Mystic Bayou really is what it's come to mean to me, it's for every-body. We have to keep treating it that way."

Jillian and Sonja went silent for a moment, blinking in confusion at this rare show of sentimentality from their supervisor.

"Sorry," Alex muttered.

"No, that was surprisingly inspirational," Sonja said.

"We should put that on a card," Jillian added, smirking.

Sonja shook her head. "Too schmaltzy. Even for Hallmark."

"Are you two *ever* going to stop giving me shit?" Alex sighed, leaning back in his chair.

The scary thing was they shook their heads in unison while saying, "No."

They burst out laughing, before Jillian finally said, "Of course, Alex. Mystic Bayou is home. And if it became home to a bunch of hyper-functional misfits like us, it will work for everybody. It's wrong to try to keep it for ourselves."

Sonja nodded. "She's right."

Alex threw his arms up. "I just said the exact same thing."

Sonja pointed to Jillian. "Yes, but hers was less mockable."

Alex rolled his eyes.

"Speaking of Hallmark, why is there a Post-It Note that says 'Send Dad birthday card' with a question mark on it?" Jillian asked. "Is there a reason you shouldn't send your dad a birthday card? Does he hate his birthday? Does he not know when it is? Do you not want to ruin the surprise?"

"We've talked about you reading things on people's desks," Sonja whispered. "Even if your ability to read other people's handwriting upside down is *really* impressive."

"It's a *lime green* Post-It!" Jillian whispered back. "And the question mark is in bold! Like he traced it ten times. What was I supposed to do?"

Alex glanced down at the green note in question. He'd traced it about a dozen times, but Jillian was close. Oh, well, he should have known better than to leave important Post-Its out on his desk. And while he didn't often share personal stuff with his coworkers, Sonja and Jillian had shared so much with him about their lives. It was their way of showing trust. Maybe he should show some in return?

He cleared his throat. "My father and I aren't exactly on the best of terms. I don't know if he would want to hear from me on his birthday."

Jillian reached over the desk and gave him a tentative pat on the hand. "I know the feeling."

"Alex, do you want a relationship with your parents?" Sonja asked.

"With my mother? Yes," he said. "I'm not sure about anything else. I call them once a week, but my dad doesn't ever... We haven't talked in a long time."

"Well, maybe you hold off on the card," Sonja suggested. "I don't know, think some positive thoughts or something, try to manifest some response from your parents to let you know where to go from here? Just don't stress out so much that you punish innocent office supplies."

"Or if you don't think there's anything to salvage, you don't *have* to keep trying," Jillian said. "I stopped sending my parents cards years ago."

Alex nodded. "Thanks, can we get back to new business?"

"OK, onto the shipping-and-supply issue," Sonja said, ticking an item off her precious meeting agenda.

"No progress," Alex admitted.

Jillian simply stared at him, because like himself, she couldn't fathom that Alex was failing so miserably. "I'm starting to suspect magical interference."

Sonja arched a dark brow. "Really?

"Well, you're not just dealing with trucking companies, you're dealing with trucking companies run by *magique*, based in New Orleans," Jillian protested. "The chances of magic or some other supernatural stuff at work here is pretty high."

"You think a bunch of trucking companies have gotten together to put some sort of curse on me because they don't like the way I'm rewarding a contract for the League?" Alex asked, waggling his hand. "Seems like a stretch."

"Couldn't we just buy our own trucks? Surely, the League has a division for that," Jillian said. "There has to be a 'department of secretive transportation and/or secretive energy beaming like something out of *Star Trek*?'"

Alex chuckled. "I'm not allowed to say whether beaming technology exists due to the multiple NDAs I have signed. But what I can tell you is the League's trucking fleet is busy distributing copies of your book. And after the Eustace Cornwell incident, a lot of the League's attention has been re-allocated to PR efforts. The people at headquarters have their hands full, so we're on our own."

"And we're under actual government scrutiny now that they've acknowledged we exist," Sonja reasoned. "Hiring local companies for our business instead of splashing more cash around can only help with those PR efforts, right?"

Alex replied, "Something like that."

"Wait, is the League going to have to do mundane things like explaining their spending decisions to the public?" Jillian asked.

When Alex nodded, Jillian burst out laughing, bending at the waist and waving her hand in front of her face as if she couldn't breathe. She wheezed, "Sorry. I know it's wrong to find the misfortune of your employer to be freaking hilarious, but…"

"No, I get it," Alex coughing to cover his own chuckle. "The League has had it coming for a while, probably. But it will mean we'll have to be a little more creative in our problem-solving."

"We can do that." Sonja nodded sharply and closed her binder, which was always the signal that the meeting was over. "And now that our official business is concluded, we have something personal and off-agenda to discuss with you."

Jillian lowered her brows into a more serious expression. "Oh, right, we have a bone to pick with you."

"I think we already went personal and off-agenda with your upside-down Post-It reading!" Alex exclaimed.

"Well, with all of us living so close together, the personal and the professional are bound to get all mixed up. And you would be bored if we were predictable," Sonja said, blithely. "So, we hear that you had a bit of an issue with Eva. And that surprised me, after the conversation we had at the pie shop about her."

Alex sighed, "So she told you everything?"

"Called an official family meeting and everything, after she spilled to Jon," Sonja said.

"It's so exciting," Jillian said, bouncing in her seat, her good spirits returned. "If she agrees to an interview, I'm going to write so many journal articles! I've never met a—"

Sonja interrupted her friend with a swift gesture. "Jillian, we agreed to let Eva talk to Alex herself. He has to make the official report, remember?"

Jillian cleared her throat, her demeanor much more serious now. "Right. But we wanted to let you know, that if this was some ill-conceived flex to show her that you have authority over her—"

"What?" Alex exclaimed. "I would never do that!"

"We *know*, which is why I thought it was weird that you would approach her as a League official and not just a regular person," Sonja said. "Maybe you didn't mean for it to intimidate or scare her, or even make her consider leaving town, but that's what happened."

"What!" Alex exclaimed.

Eva couldn't leave town. He didn't want her to leave. He didn't want to take her away from her friends or her business. *He* would leave Mystic Bayou before she had to abandon the home she'd found.

"Stop saying 'what' when you know exactly what I'm talking about. And let's not even go into whether you were supposed to be looking at her records in the first place," Jillian added. "I'll just assume that you have access to files I couldn't dream of. The point is, you scared her. And if you're interested in Eva, like Sonja seems to think you are, you have some apologizing to do."

"Some might even say 'groveling,'" Sonja noted brightly.

Jillian grinned. "Groveling never hurt anyone."

Alex blew a long breath out of his nose and stood. "Excuse me. I have to go buy a banana cream pie."

"You know, in any other town, that would be a strange way to leave a room?" Sonja murmured as Alex strode out of Jillian's office.

———

EVEN AT THE DOOR, the Carmody and Boudreaux boat shop smelled of motor oil and something that was uniquely Eva. A clean, not-overly-sweet scent that reminded Alex of a trip his family had taken to Biloxi when he was kid. That probably sounded wrong, but he swore he could smell it as he approached the workshop door, bakery box in hand.

He was relieved to see that Jon wasn't present when he knocked at the open door. If he was going to do the amount of groveling Eva deserved, he didn't want an audience. But, then again, Eva probably deserved an audience, too.

She was there, bent over a tidy worktable piecing together some mechanical thing he didn't quite understand. She was wearing those overalls, tied around her waist, revealing strong shoulders under a thin-strapped tank top. Her hands moved in a hypnotic dance around the metal, clicking and twisting the gears until they made a sound that she seemed to find satisfactory.

His brain insisted that should not have been nearly as sexy as it was, but he told his brain to shut up and mind its own business.

She turned suddenly and her mouth twisted into a line that indicated she was not happy to see him. Her body seemed to sag in exhaustion, and she carefully set the metal bits aside.

"I'm sorry," he started.

"No, let me speak," Eva started. "You're right. My last name isn't Boudreaux. It's Orebender. I'm only telling you this because I don't want you to go to the League and stir up a bunch of paperwork that can make my life more complicated here. I've told Jon all about my past. It wasn't easy, but I told him. And while I appreciate that you gave me the time to do it, I'm still pissed at you for making me, if that makes sense."

"It does and I'm—"

"Nope, no, I need you to let me get all of this out before you say anything, or I'll never finish it." She cut him off with a swipe of her hand, which she then wiped with her bandana of the day – dark blue and printed with pouting stars? He wondered briefly if her bandanas could be used as some sort of mood meter, but she had such long elegant fingers that he caught himself watching her perform even that simple act in a way that would probably make her uncomfortable.

"I'm a gnome," Eva said.

He opened his mouth to speak and then closed it. The words just hung there between them, waiting in vain for Alex to process them. How was he supposed to respond? People didn't just go around saying things like "I'm a gnome." But this was Mystic

Bayou and one of his closest neighbors was a forest creature who could tickle people to death, so...

Nope, still did not compute.

He couldn't seem to produce words, only stare, trying to reconcile what he knew about gnomes – which was almost nothing, now that he thought about it – with the tall, beautiful decidedly-not-bearded woman standing in front of him.

Come on, Alex, say something, his brain commanded him. *Something that inspires reassurance after she's shared this background information that she's been so careful to conceal.*

But all he managed to say was, "Er, come again?"

Oh, real smooth, you idiot. A regular James freaking Bond. No wonder the last girl turned you down for a mermaid.

"A *gnome*," she said a second time, her irritation growing. "I mean, it's not really what we call ourselves, but it's how other *magique* know us. Hell, you could probably ask your bosses about my family. We've made pieces for the League bigwigs for years, to honor promotions or as gifts to smooth over diplomatic issues... Wait, no, don't do that. I don't want anyone at League headquarters to know I'm here. Dammit. This isn't coming out like I'd hoped."

"Wait, gnomes? Like the cute little lawn statues with the pointy hats and rosy cheeks?" And for some reason he would never understand, Alex held his hand up over his head, like she'd never seen a freaking gnome statue.

"OK, that's some bullshit," she growled, crossing her arms over her chest. "We don't even know where those stupid garden statues came from. It was probably the damn goblins. They just love to give us grief."

So, he'd only managed to produce one sentence and it was a sentence that offended her. His brain wasn't talking to him anymore.

Eva was still fuming and somehow, the southern accent faded, and she sounded almost European? Something between Greek and Slavic and seething mad. "I mean, it doesn't even make *sense*. Pointy hats are *super* impractical when you live underground. And beards aren't exactly a plus when you're working with molten metal. And the shortest among us are six feet tall. We have super-human strength, and our senses are more acute than any were-creature you've ever come across. They have to be when you spend most of your time in the dark. We're not jolly or cherubic in any way. In fact, we're descendants of elemental creatures that pre-date most known folklore. You know, my grandpa always insisted that our family was the inspiration for how Hephaestus was depicted in Greek mythology."

Alex held up a hand and worked to produce the words, "Wait, I have questions. So many questions."

She clapped a hand over her face. "Apparently, that's the standard response for League higher-ups. I thought Jillian was going to set Jon's whole living room on fire with her delighted squeals/flames."

"Yeah, she's going to spend a lot of time interviewing you," Alex said. He set the pie box on the worktable and sat on the stool nearby. He felt like he was able to breathe for the first time since he'd found the inconsistencies in Eva's history. He'd been so worried that she'd come to the Bayou to cause problems, but now, he could fulfill his obligations to League regulations just by snooping around in some League financial records to confirm her story. The League kept receipts for*ever.* Eva's name probably appeared on a few if she'd been involved in any way – then he could drop the whole thing. So, he'd just created an enormous amount of tension with her for no real reason...

Shit.

He'd like to say he was normally better at this sort of thing, but he hadn't successfully wooed a woman since he'd arrived in Mystic Bayou. Maybe this was his own personal rift? Only instead of leaking otherworldly energy that changed people at a DNA level, it just made Alex incapable of connecting with women? Or maybe he was just not ready for an adult relationship, like Lizzie had said... in the letter delivered by her divorce attorney. He had, in fact, used the word "wooed," which probably wasn't a great sign for him, in terms of emotional development.

"So, Jon didn't bring up the pointy hats when you talked to him, huh?" he asked, desperate to fill the awkward verbal space.

"No, he didn't," she said, eying him pointedly. "He was more concerned about why I felt the need to hide it."

"Well, why *did* you feel the need to hide it?" Alex asked.

She reached into a mini fridge under the worktable and pulled out two bottles of water, then climbed onto the stool next to him. She offered him the bottle, but he noticed she was careful not to touch his hand. It made his chest hurt, how cautious she felt she needed to be around him. He'd made a mistake, approaching her like he did, and it was going to take work to fix what he'd broken.

"So, we're going to need to go back to the beginning," she sighed. "There are gnomes all over the world, but my father's family in particular comes from under the mountains near the Mediterranean. We live underground in complex warrens, but when we want to travel, we make our way through a series of tunnels. And spending so much time underground, we're very familiar with gems, gold, all sorts of precious things that can be dug from under rock and dirt. Some gnome families specialize in iron work, others in silver-smithing. Actually, there's a very odd gnome family out west that loves dinosaur bones? Now that I think about it, they have beards, but they're certainly not typical. Still, they've made some really interesting discoveries–"

She seemed to realize he was staring at her, brow furrowed. She shrugged. "Sorry, the point is that it doesn't make for fun fairy tale hijinks. We're artists. And we live for that art, no matter what form we practice. My family are some of the premiere gem-setters in the supernatural world. In the last few centuries, we've established a sort of jewelry empire, providing special commissioned pieces for *magique* of all sorts. Of course, humans have managed to 'acquire' some of those pieces, and they've ended up in the hands of royal families or worse, human museums, where people can't even wear them."

"Sorry about that. As a species, we sort of suck," Alex said.

"No!" Eva shook her head and the façade of frustration seemed to break. Joy and warmth seeped through the cracks, and he could see the Eva he knew. She reached forward and placed her hand on his wrist, for the briefest of moments. "No, I mean, yes, in a lot of ways, humans are the worst. But your ingenuity, the things that you can do *without* magical gifts, that's what drew me to the surface. Well, that and the need to get away from my family. That's why I lied. The fake name, the fake history."

"The fake accent," he noted, making her wince.

"Yeah, although the accent has become completely natural at this point. I had to create a whole new person for my life here, accent included. I didn't want my family to find me," she said softly.

He reached out to touch *her* hand, but stopped short, realizing that she might not want that. "Do you need help? We have programs at the League, for people who are running from harmful situations."

"No, no, nothing like that," she said quickly. His whole body seemed to flush when she caught his fingers in hers. Was he getting dizzy? He felt like he might be tilting off the stool, but he fought to focus on what she was saying to anchor himself. "It's just that they don't understand why I live my life the way I do. And I am tired of trying to explain it to them. They think my talents are supposed to be used to benefit them and they don't understand why I'd rather work on something as uninspired as machines. And I just want to be left alone. That's why I have an assumed name and identity, which as you know, is probably going to be made legal in the coming year, in order help the *magique* assimilate into the human world after the Eustace Cornwell Incident."

He tried not to avoid her gaze. He really did.

"I'm not doing anything wrong. I wouldn't do anything to hurt anyone. I just want to live here and do my work and be left alone," Eva said.

"How long ago did you leave your family?" Alex asked, shifting so his knees were closer to hers. He didn't want to scare her away, but he didn't want to be so far from her. She tolerated his minor intrusion into her personal space, and he chose to see that as a good sign.

"Oh, not long, just two hundred years or so," Eva said.

He would not question how old she was. If growing up with the "guess your weight and age" showmen at the carnival had taught him anything, it was that women of any species did not appreciate that.

"Do you have any reason to believe that your family has tracked you here and are surveilling you?" he asked, thinking of the black truck he'd seen around town, the one that seemed to be following her.

She hesitated and then shook her head again. "No, I don't think they would be subtle, looking for me. I would definitely hear crashing sounds and indignant shouting."

He thought about telling her about the truck, but he had no proof beyond a sense of foreboding, over a truck, one of dozens of similar trucks in the parish. So, he decided to file away those concerns until he was sure they actually meant something. He worried that he'd lost so much credibility with her that any warning he gave her would be ignored.

Eva squeezed his fingers lightly, capturing his attention. "Now, I need to know, why did you do it? Why did you dig into my past?"

He jerked his shoulders, trying to appear casual. "I just wanted to know you better."

She snorted derisively. "Try again."

He frowned at her. He turned so they were facing each other, staring directly into her deep earthen eyes. "So here is my apology. I'm sorry, truly. I don't know how much Jillian and Sonja and the rest have told you about the last couple of years around here, but when people show up with fake backgrounds, bad things tend to happen. I overreacted because I have a lot to lose here, but I hate to think that what I've lost is the chance to be close to you, to talk to you."

"Well, I'm not going to openly shun you or anything," she scoffed. She slid off of the stool and stepped away, putting more distance between them. "It's nice that you want to look out for the people around here, to keep them safe. I just wish that you'd done it in a way that didn't violate my privacy and disrupt my pie consumption."

"Don't paint me as some sort of martyr for the community, Eva. I also looked into your background because you're interesting and beautiful and I wanted to know more about you, which I realize now is probably a little inappropriate. And then, when I saw that everything didn't quite add up, I panicked and went all official on you. It was wrong on a lot of levels," Alex said.

She stared at him. "Look, I'm not going to sue the League or anything, you don't have to make up some story about being interested in me. It's a little insulting."

"I *am* interested in you. Why do you have such a hard time believing that?" he asked, following her as she stalked towards Jon's tool station.

She laughed, and it was a bitter, hollow sound. "Oh, come on, Alex, it's not like we... move in the same circles. I have a collection of novelty bandanas because my hands are always covered in grease. I don't have a formal education, except for engine repair classes. You're a lawyer! You work with the League! You're *fancy* like Sonja, always spotless, always match-y. I mean, does a professional stylist do your hair every morning or did you attend some six-week seminar on how to make it do that?"

"The way you're describing me sounds a little superficial and shallow," he replied.

She didn't immediately object or claim that wasn't what she meant... which stung.

"I'm just saying people like you don't find people like me 'interesting' and 'beautiful.' People in my *own* community didn't call me interesting or beautiful," she said, her cheeks flushing as she backed toward Jon's worktable. "Which is fine. I've come to terms with the fact that I grew up surrounded by people who... weren't ideal in terms of emotions or affection. But I would rather you didn't try to cover up some administrative screw-up with this pretend *story*. Unlike you, I've been rejected. I can handle it."

He scoffed, but when she didn't laugh, his jaw dropped. "Wait? You think I've never been rejected?"

She backed away, bumping into the table behind her. "Well, no."

"Well, I think *that's* superficial and shallow, to assume that about me," he shot back as he followed her. He carefully placed his hands on the table, on either side of her hips, and hoped the fact that he was looking up at her reduced the "cornering" factor of the position. "Just because I look a certain way doesn't mean my life is any smoother or less disappointing than anyone else's. You don't know me very well, so I feel like I should make it clear. I don't play games. I may not be able to tell everybody the whole truth when it comes to work, but I don't lie, especially not when it comes to people's feelings, especially if it comes to *your* feelings."

She was staring down at him and the fact that she hadn't smacked him with one of the readily available wrenches gave him the boldness required to press his mouth to hers. Her lips were so *warm* and tasted of ginger and spice. How could a simple kiss feel like coming home?

He groaned into her mouth softly and he felt her chuckle against his lips. She trailed a hand over his cheek, and he broke away from her mouth to lean into the caress like a cat. Her hands on his skin just felt so *good,* not just in the physical sense, but because it was *her* touching him, her hands on him. She was staring down at him, lips parted and breathing heavily, her eyes glazed.

He stretched upwards and pressed his mouth to hers, dragging his fingers through that fascinating bronze hair. He lost himself in her, her breath, her mouth, the smell of her skin. She shuddered against him and he smiled, pleased that he could affect her like that. She pulled him close one last time and then sort of slid her hands under his arms. She lifted him gently, placing him a few steps away from her.

Alex interpreted this as a need for space and took another step away from her. The moment, as delicious as it had been, was over. He cleared his throat and decided to change the subject to something neutral, something that wouldn't make him seem desperate to determine if he had any chance at another kiss.

OK, he commanded his brain, *come up with something clever, casual and not at all creepy*.

But what came out of his mouth was, "So, did you and Jarvis Luckwell have that drink?"

His brain had abandoned him, clearly considering him a lost cause.

Eva's face went blank. "What?"

Cursing his runaway brain, he said, "It's just that he seemed so keen on you, the other night, asking you out for that drink."

She burst out laughing, a rich, musical sound that persuaded him that maybe his brain decided on a second chance. "Oh, my gods, no. No. Leprechauns – Jarvis in particular – seem to pride themselves on being all tricky and jovial, without realizing it makes them come across as being happy-go-lucky sociopaths. That's not exactly boyfriend material, not that I'm necessarily looking for boyfriend material, but still. Also, his name is Jarvis. I can't see myself yelling 'Jarvis' in the throes of passion."

He was so caught between the erotic image of Eva in the throes of passion and then, revulsion at that image possibly involving Jarvis that he couldn't speak. He could only blink.

Eva bit her lip. "It's possible I just said too much."

"No!" he said quickly, holding up his hands. "No, that's good."

"Why is that good?"

"Well, because you should date people that you like," he said, clearing his throat. "Not happy-go-lucky sociopaths with unappealing names. And I would like to take you to dinner, some place nice, as an apology and just because I want to go to dinner with you. Some place nice. Did I mention that already?"

She tilted her head, watching him as he pulled at his collar. A slow smile spread over her face. "Do I make you nervous?"

"Possibly?" he suggested, swallowing heavily. "Yes, yes, you do."

"I like that, maybe more than I should." Smirking, she nodded at the bakery box where he'd left it on her table. "Is that for me?"

He pulled her hand gently until they reached the pie box and offered it to her with a flourish. "It's an apology pie, which makes it even better than a verbal apology, in my humble opinion. And not to make you feel obligated to accept it, but you don't want to know what sort of imported spices I had to get through customs to persuade Siobhan to sell me a whole pie that she didn't specifically assign to someone."

She opened the box and gave him a look that warmed him all the way down to his toes. "It's banana cream."

"Well, yeah, that's the pie you were eating when I interrupted you," he said.

She grinned at him and pulled him close, kissing him with even more force than before, stealing his breath. She gave him one last little kiss and even rubbed the tip of her nose against his, which he enjoyed far more than he'd expected.

"Dinner sounds very nice, but I'd rather stay in," she told him. "If you ever wanted to come by my house, that might be nice, too."

"I'm free now," he said quickly.

"I'm working *now*," she said, laughing. "But call me sometime. I'm sure you found my number through your scary League resources."

"Yes, I did." He practically stumbled away from her.

"Hey, Alex?"

Hearing his name on her lips sent a little shiver down his spine. He turned to face her.

"Just for the record, when you say, 'imported spices,' you don't mean drugs, right?" Eva asked.

His lips pulled back into a grimace. "You know, I'm not entirely sure."

———

Jon was waiting for Alex when he walked out of the boat shop, sitting on the hood of his SUV. And he was eating a slice of banana cream pie.

Alex whipped his head back to the shop, where Eva sat on one of the stools, eating her own slice. "How – how did you? Time and space have rules, you know!"

Jon shrugged, chewing on his pie. "Mystic Bayou."

"But– "

"Mystic Bayou," Jon said again. He hopped up and closed the boat shop door.

"Why are you doing that?" Eva called from inside.

"Because we're going to talk about you!" Jon yelled through the door.

Eva put up very little argument, simply yelling back, "Fine!"

Jon leveled Alex with a look, all humor gone from his expression. "Before you go I need to make one thing clear – Eva may be stronger physically than both of us put together, but you can hurt her just like anybody else. And if you hurt her, you'll have me to deal with. And yeah, maybe that's not terribly intimidating, considering all I can do is swim real fast at you, but you'll also have a pissed-off dragon and a bear to contend with. They'll mess you up. And then they'll hand you over to the ladies. And when *they're* done, there won't be enough left of you to bury in a shoebox."

Alex considered that for a moment.

"Did I go too far?" Jon asked, looking guilty for a moment.

Alex chuckled and clapped a hand on Jon's shoulder. "Nah, I'm glad that Eva has people who care about her enough to threaten me with multiple felonies."

"Damn straight, we will."

6

———

EVA

ZED'S garage was much like Zed, a little disorganized, but clean and welcoming.

That was a super-weird thought to have about a man while tuning up his motorcycle, but her whole week was turning out pretty weird. Alex was like a handsome grenade tossed into the life she'd built, forcing her to re-align pretty much everything very quickly. Fortunately, the response from her friends – that she'd basically lied to them about every single aspect of herself since she'd met them – had been pretty minimal. Other than Jillian freaking out entirely at the idea of learning about a heretofore-unknown-to-her species of *magique*, and Sonja informing her that they weren't worried because Lia had "scanned" her when they'd first met, using her special ability to read emotions, and picked up nothing but nerves and good intentions. Eva wasn't super-offended by this. It was just a matter of common sense. If you had a gift that could protect you, you used it.

But Zed and Bael, of course, asked questions about her family that she couldn't fully answer, concerned that she needed protection. Sonja offered to undo any administrative damage Alex might have done to Eva's carefully constructed persona while he was quote, "bumbling through the system." Jon had been far more focused on how it affected their stationary needs.

"I can file the business papers all over again to change us to Carmody and Orebender," had been his first response after she'd delivered her story, barely making it through without tears. Then he grimaced. "Oh, man, that means I'm going to have to order all new t-shirts and signs and stuff."

Oh, this sweet goofball of a man.

"Really? You're worried most about... t-shirts?" she'd asked.

"Well, Carmody and Boudreaux looks super-classy on the t-shirts." He shrugged. "But I guess Carmody and Orebender will look classy, too, though. Maybe we can keep the same font. It depends on the sizing and placement."

She hugged him tight, making him chuckle and pat her back. "No, please don't change the name or the font. I made *my* life, the life I want, with the name Boudreaux. I want that name on our business."

He shrugged. "All right, then. You got time for that airboat tune-up before we wrap up for the day?"

"You don't have any other questions for me?" Eva asked.

Jon jerked his shoulders again. "No, I mean, you obviously had your reasons for giving a fake name. Just look at Cordelia and how hard she worked to hide from her mama. And Cordy never did anything to cause any trouble. There's no reason to think you would. But if you need help, please don't hide it from us. We're here for you, Eva Orebender."

While she loved him for it, Eva wasn't about to take Jon up on that. Her family's memory was long. It didn't matter that her betrayal was hundreds of years ago, they would feel like it had only happened the week before. She wasn't about to drag the people she loved into any sort of fight involving those she left behind.

And then, of course, Alex had walked into their shop with his pie-based apology. And proceeded to make out with her. Immediately following that knee-wobbling kiss, Eva was a little ashamed of her doubts of his affections. It just seemed so unbelievable that the whole time she'd been watching him, wanting him, he'd been watching and wanting her, too. She'd had crushes before and they'd rarely worked out so simply.

Add to that, Alex wasn't *her* usual type, either. But, meddling aside, he was smart and kind. He tried to make up for what he'd done. He hadn't meant to hurt her, and when he acted, he'd acted out of concern for the people around him. So, she supposed she had to forgive him for it. She wasn't sure making out with him against her worktable was the right choice, but she couldn't go back and change that.

His lips tasted like peppermint and dirty promises, and she didn't know how to process that.

"Penny for your thoughts," a deep voice sounded behind her as she crouched by Zed's Springer Soft Tail Classic. He handed her a glass of lemonade, a departure from their usual beers, which was probably a testament to Zed wanting her to be sober while operating on his beloved bike baby, rather than poor hospitality.

"I'm just wondering why you're having me do this when you're pretty capable of keeping your bike running yourself."

Zed jerked his broad shoulders, leaning against a chest freezer where he stored a "winter's worth" of meat products. Eva didn't want to question that, either. "Eh, I figured it was a good time to have someone who actually knows what they're doing take a look."

Eva scoffed. "I've done a few of these on my own and read some books on the subject, Zed, it's not like I'm a master motor-cycle mechanic. Wait," she lifted a brow. "Why *now*?"

Zed scratched the back of his neck, looking uncomfortable. "Don't tell Dani."

Eva arched her brow. "Oh, no."

"No, nothing, bad," he swore. "But I'm thinking about selling it. You can't exactly put a baby in a side car, can ya? At least, not the way I ride. And it doesn't seem fair to Dani, having something just for me to enjoy. Especially when Dani's already throwing up every five minutes and pushing our gigantic *enfant* out of her..." He waved a hand toward his middle. "Area covered by her bathing suit. That feels like enough of a sacrifice."

She stood, putting aside her tools and hugged him. "You're a very nice man."

"Thank you."

"But this is the wrong plan," she added.

He practically squawked, "What?"

"Look, I've watched enough talk shows to know that women go through enough relationship worries when they're expecting without their well-intentioned partner piling on more. If you give up something that's so mixed in with your personality, like your bike, she's going to feel super guilty. You don't want to throw that at her while she's sleep-deprived and getting hit with all those hormones," Eva said.

He protested, "But I need to do something to show Dani how much I appreciate everything she's going through for us."

"You rubbed lavender balm into her feet the other night while all your friends watched," she cried. "That wasn't proof enough?"

He shrugged. "I'm a big gesture guy."

"Think smaller," she told him. "Also, never let your fiancé find out that you refer to her vagina as the 'area covered by her bathing suit.'"

Zed shuddered. "Well, I'm not used to discussing her parts with other people at all!"

"And that is why we're friends."

Working on the bike took no time at all, considering how Zed babied the thing. Within an hour, he was walking Eva out to her truck, tools in hand.

"I still wish you would let me pay you something," Zed insisted. "It doesn't feel right, letting you work for free on my bike."

"I have three jars of Dani's famous applesauce in my bag," she retorted. "If anything, I'm taking advantage of *you*."

"She's been canning like crazy here lately, says it reminds her of home. I think she just misses her grandma. My *maman* says it's something called 'nesting' and totally normal," Zed said, staring off into the distance, his brow furrowed. She followed his eyeline into the trees. The wrinkle of his brow was troubling. And somehow, she swore she could hear faint screams coming from the trees, like they were playing over a radio in the distance.

Zed being disturbed by anything this close to his den made the hairs on her arms stand up. She didn't see what was making him glower like that, but she felt… watched, not just observed but as if she was smack in the middle of the crosshairs on a hunter's scope.

Her breathing turned shallow and panicked. Could her parents have finally found her? Was it like speaking of the devil? She'd known, eventually, that they would find her. She just thought she had more time, after finally coming clean to her friends. And suddenly, a sharp acrid smell filled her nostrils and she gagged. "Ugh, do you smell that?"

Zed's nose wrinkled. "Yeah."

"It's like a rotten egg smell," she said, eying him carefully. "With a hint of dirty diaper."

Zed actually did the pearl-clutching gesture on the front of his dark t-shirt. "Hey, don't look at me. I may be big and loud, but *maman* raised me not to be completely disgusting."

"Maybe it's the swamp?"

"Well, 'rotten egg farts' is usually how people describe the smell of the Devil's Armpit," Zed shook his head, still staring into the trees. "But we're too far away to smell it here. It's part of the reason my great-great-great-great-great-granddaddy chose this spot – no stink."

Eva frowned, ignoring the fact that the number of "greats" for Zed's ancestor changed every time he told the story. "I'm not so much worried about the smell as this weird feeling that someone is watching."

"I don't like this," he said. "I'm calling Bael. It's part of an agreement we all made to report weird shit as soon as it happens. We even signed papers."

She wanted to protest, to insist it wasn't that big of a deal, because she didn't want to have to explain what she'd left out when she'd told everybody about her past – the parts that left her feeling ashamed. She just wasn't ready. So instead, she just nodded and loaded her tools into her truck.

After their shared discomfort, Zed tried to insist on following her home to make sure she arrived safe, but she didn't feel right, leaving Dani unprotected when the threat they'd felt was close to home. She called him the moment she was safely inside the house and delivered the promised "safe word," which was "rotten egg fart."

And then she closed all of the curtains, shutting herself off from the view of the woods and water that she normally loved so much, even at night. She just had this horrible, sinking dread that if she looked out the window, she would see some awful creature breathing against the glass. If that meant she lived inside a box for a night, so be it. It was a pretty nice box.

Speaking of which.

She realized she was tiptoeing back to her bedroom, which made no sense. It wasn't like she needed to sneak up on what she was seeking out. She rolled her eyes at herself and slid her arms under her bed. She wasn't exactly a master carpenter, but she'd managed to build a compartment underneath her bedframe that looked like it was original to the furniture, meant to support the over-sized upholstered headboard. She popped the compartment open and took out the chest that contained her previous life.

The iron casket was a gift from her mother's branch of the family, iron workers who'd inscribed the chest with runes explaining Eva's lineage, how her family had sprung from the Earth and made the most of its gifts. It had been months since she'd looked at it, having tucked it away after moving in and leaving it there. It was as if she thought that she could pretend that time never existed, if she just didn't think about it. But it was always there, lurking under her bed like the damn Tell-Tale Heart.

Inhaling deeply through her nose, Eva turned the series of wheels and levers hidden in the design, like a combination lock. Only a member of her mother's family would know how to open it, but she still felt the need to hide it. Clever locks didn't prevent someone from using dynamite on the hinges.

She carried the chest into her living room, where the light of the lamps was brightest. If she was going to put herself through this, she was going to view the contents at their best. The electric lights weren't exactly the fires of the family forge, but they made the jewels glitter with an almost supernatural gleam.

She'd always been charmed by the glimmer of light across the surface of precious stones. It still didn't make sense to her that such beautiful things came from her imagination, her hands. While her true calling was mechanical, she'd had an aptitude for setting jewels. Even as she carefully removed the interior drawer, her collection spilled out onto her coffee table like a frozen rainbow.

This was just a tiny fraction of her collection, the best bits of her designs. Her mother considered her style a bit too literal, making copies of everyday objects out of gems and metal, but she enjoyed making things so realistic that the eye felt fooled for just a moment. Besides, hadn't Eva bowed to her mother's demands that she stick to the family's old-fashioned methods? Eva had used ancient tools and fire rather than metallurgy that had been considered cutting edge in the *Roman Empire*. She'd felt stifled, but she'd done it, because it just hadn't been worth the argument, when gems weren't her true passion.

Her first piece had been a cuff bracelet made of silver, set with emeralds in the shape of a leaf. The problem was that it wasn't identifiable as any leaf species found in nature. She'd left it on her father's worktable when she left. She hoped he still had it. She'd gotten better over the years and her collection showed it.

She never wore any of these pieces. She rarely took them out, in fact. But she held onto them, to remind her of how she got her start. It was sort of like an artist carrying around a sketchbook of their early work. Hers just happened to be really, really sparkly.

There was a diadem of gold and ruby that made the wearer look like she was wearing a crown of rose petals. There was a citrine-and-onyx brooch fashioned in the shape of a monarch butterfly so detailed, her father swore he was afraid to touch it, because it might get frightened and fly away. Eva was particularly proud of the cloak pin shaped like a dagger, with pearls in the handle, that was sharp enough to cut the skin... which she supposed just made it a dagger. Hmm.

Feeling the slick surfaces of the stones, the weight of the metal against her skin, settled her in a way she wished it didn't. She told herself it was the appreciation for the craftsmanship, not the value of what she held in her hand. But yes, there was a certain security in knowing that if things got really desperate, she could sell the contents of that toolbox and be quite comfortable. But after the Ocean's Eye, she didn't think she could go through that again.

Beneath all of the chest's tiny drawers, Eva caught a glimpse of the compartment where her pick-axe was stored. After her initial training, she'd rarely actually mined for jewels or ore. It was more ceremonial than anything else, a polished maple handle with a head comprised of bronze. Her father preferred gold, of course, but pure gold would be too damn soft if she'd actually needed to use it. And while the family produced decoration, they were definitely practical people. There was no point in owning something you couldn't use. It may not have "sparked joy", but it definitely could have been used in a pinch. In case of zombies, or something.

It felt very natural to reach for it when the knock sounded at her door. It felt right in her hand, balanced and ready to attack that monster she'd imagined at the window. She was surprised at how much abject fear she could feel after all these years. Her hands were numb and cold. She could barely feel her face, she was so scared. She couldn't even think. Something was on the other side of her door, and she didn't know what it wanted or what it intended.

"Eva?" Alex's voice called. "Are you in there? Are you OK?"

"Alex?"

Relief coursed through her with a warmth that helped her feel her face again. She jerked the door open, to find Alex standing on her doorstep, a concerned expression on his face. She remembered just a second too late that she was still holding a comically large pick-axe. With a speed that belied her size, she stashed it behind the curtains over her front window.

Given Alex's lack of alarm, she was pretty sure he didn't see it.

"What are you doing here?"

"Um, Zed called and asked me to check in on you," Alex said.

"Why didn't he just call Jon?"

"Jon's not picking up. Apparently, this is his and Lia's night to 'run free?'" Alex said, shrugging. "I don't really know what that means, but I don't think Jon can put a phone anywhere on his body that he would want to use it later – what the fuck!"

He was looking behind her with an expression of absolute alarm and for the briefest moment, she thought maybe that unknown creature was, in fact, crouching in her living room. But when she turned to follow his line of sight, she realized she'd been so caught up in her anxiety that she forgot that her collection was still spread out on the table when she opened the door.

Alex was almost green with panic. "Eva, you didn't go into Bael's treasure cave, did you? I mean, I know it's tempting, and this stuff is beautiful, but dragons take that shit *so seriously*–"

Eva burst out laughing "No, no, no! I know better than to go near a dragon's horde. I don't even know where Bael's cave is."

"Oh, thank god," Alex sighed, putting his hands on her shoulder. "I like you a lot, but I don't know if I could save you from a pissed off dragon. I would try, but I would probably get set on fire in the process."

She cackled, bent over at the waist laughing. When she rose, he was beaming at her, and that expression of contentment on his face made her feel warmed all the way through. She put her hand on his shoulder. "Relax. This is just my personal collection of jewelry. Things I made, back when I lived with my family."

His jaw dropped. "Wait, you *made* this?"

"I told you, my family are jewelers," she reminded him.

"Right. In my panic, I did not make that connection." He

flushed red, but a moment later curiosity seemed to take hold. He took a step towards the table and then turned back to her. "Can I take a closer look?"

"Yes, thanks for asking." He was very careful not to touch, she noticed. He would look closely at one piece or another but ask her to pick it up and turn it over to show him. He didn't look at them with the gleam of greed in his eyes, as she'd seen from so many humans before. He looked at them with the interest and awe of someone staring at priceless art.

It spoke well of him, she thought, not just as a person who spent a lot of time around *magique* and was aware of the cultural mores, but as someone who didn't want to make her uncomfortable. If she hadn't already warmed to him, that would have done it.

"They're beautiful," he breathed, a smile spreading over his face like a sunrise. "Look at – you *made this?* But you build boat engines. How do those two things go together?"

"I happen to *like* boat engines," she said primly.

"But you could be working for some huge jeweler as a custom designer or something."

"And you could be working for some fancy law firm in a big city," she countered. Now that the show-and-tell portion of the evening seemed to be over, she packed the pieces away in the casket. She watched his face while she did so, waiting for the avaricious glint to show up as she took the shiny prizes out of his reach. But if he felt anything beyond appreciation, he was a masterful actor.

He thought about that and nodded. "Point taken. Wait, so you have all this, and you rolled into town in a pick-up that could have belonged to my grandpa?"

It took her a moment to understand what he was implying and she scoffed. "I couldn't *sell* them! They're personal. It would be like selling your finger-paintings from kindergarten."

"Your finger-paintings and my finger-paintings are very different," he snorted. She rose and got two beers out of her fridge. She gestured to her backdoor without thinking. She always drank her beer on the dock behind her house. It was habit. Alex had made her so comfortable so quickly, she'd forgotten about the unnerving smell and presence outside Zed's house. How was he able to do that?

He grinned happily, following her out to the dock. She sat down, mentally scanning the space around them, but she didn't sense anything off-putting. She didn't even sense the weird egg smell she caught outside Zed's. So, little by little, she relaxed. Without overwhelming fear clogging her senses, it was a remarkably romantic setting, the drinks, the insects chirping, the moon shining down over the water.

"It smells nice out here. Not nearly as swampy," he noted.

"That's because of Jon. Selkies call the ocean to them, wherever they are, so all that beautiful blue Gulf water travels all the way up the river to his place. I just enjoy the side effects," she said.

He took a sip of his stout and blanched. She realized that Alex might be more used to some of the IPAs Jon favored, which she refused to have in her house. She suddenly felt embarrassed that she was so ill-prepared to host someone without her tastes.

"I can make you some coffee or tea. I think I have some bourbon," she said.

"This is fine," he rasped.

"You know you can't tell anybody about this, all right?"

"That your beer is too intense for me?" he asked. She lifted a brow at him and lost the teasing expression. "No, no. I understand I can't talk about the jewelry. I don't want every creep in the parish breaking in here like something out of the *Goonies*. I would never put you in danger, Eva."

"Thank you."

"I know you said you were a jeweler before, but I guess I didn't picture pieces that were so elaborate, so *royal*. I guess I was picturing heavy silver rings and beaten arm cuffs or something. Nothing this... exquisite, that's the only word for it," Alex said.

Now it was her turn to blush. Just the word coming out of his mouth, "exquisite," was enough to make her want to fan her face. That was super-normal, right?

"I'm not knocking what you're doing now, but how did you go from making things like that to fixing boats?" he said, sipping his drink and wincing. "I deserved that."

She chuckled, her expression turning pensive. "So, there is no Career Day for gnomes. No matter what your family's specialty is, *that's* what you're going to do with the rest of your life. Orebenders start mining as soon as they're strong enough to lift a pick-axe. When you've proven that you appreciate the mines, you're moved to the foundry and the forges. And once you've proven you're smart enough not to waste anything of value, you're moved to the workshop. You learn basic design, how to cut and set the gems. And once you prove you have the knack, you're moved to the 'big show,' the master's workshop."

"What if you don't have the knack?"

"You rise as high as you're capable and you stay there," Eva explained. "Most of us are so devoted to the success of the family that resentments... Well, I won't say they don't happen, but most of us find contentment wherever we end up. It's not a perfect system, but as a rule, we're pretty community-minded. I was an anomaly, I guess."

He frowned. "Because you didn't have the knack?"

"I moved to the master's workshop faster than any Orebender in the family archives," she said with a smirk. "I had the aptitude, but little passion. After a few years, I got bored."

"Oh, so you're one of those infuriating people who doesn't like doing something that they're really good at."

She pursed her lips. "Yeah, I guess I am. Some League dignitary gave my father a pocket watch as a goodwill gesture. I started playing around with it and realized that I like re-arranging the mechanical bits a lot better than smelting or cutting gems. Don't get me wrong, I loved looking at those shiny bits of rock and seeing what they could *become*, the way the metal would bend to my will and change into something out of a queen's dream. And yeah, they were pretty. But a lot of things in this world are pretty. A necklace can loop around your neck, make you feel beautiful, but it can't get a dying man to the hospital or sew a dress together."

"When then the Industrial Revolution came and there were all these machines out in the world, making life easier, doing things for people. Sometimes, when people throw things away, they go below the surface. I kept finding these little machines that people had discarded and I would take them apart only to put them back together again. I *understood* them. I knew what they needed to be more, to be better. Yes, I was good at making pretties from gold and gems, but I didn't go to sleep thinking about bracelets and diadems. My last thought at night and my first thought in the morning was about gears and sockets – which doesn't exactly speak well of the men I was spending time around, I guess.

"I asked my family if I could live above ground for a while, maybe take an apprenticeship with a human machinist. But they laughed. For one thing, humans at the time didn't believe it was proper or even possible for a woman to work with metal. Not even blacksmithing. And for another, it simply wasn't *done* for our family to abandon jewelry, not for any other interest. I snuck out to human libraries and studied designs for every machine I could find."

"The Industrial Revolution?" he asked, his voice cracking.

She smirked again. "Yes, I'm almost six hundred years old. Is that a problem?"

"No." He shuddered. "It's kind of hot, to be honest. So, wait, you went above the surface? That must have been a huge break from what you were used to."

"We live underground, but we're not allergic to sunlight or anything. Some of us even have homes above ground for vacations, the same way you might think of having a beach house. Anyway—" She shook her head. And while she knew it was unfair to skip so many chapters in her story, the next thing she said was, "Eventually, I had to leave. For my own happiness, for my own sanity, I ran away. I sort of drifted around until I found my way to London. I hid in an abandoned workshop in Whitechapel for years, learning how cogs fit together. I was fascinated by every bit of the process, building things that were functional and had the potential to do *anything*. And when cars came along? I don't think I slept for two years, taking engines apart and putting them together. Falling in love with boats, that's more of a recent thing, a fancy, if you will. They've made watercrafts so interesting in the last few decades. I might turn my attention to electric cars next, depending on how things go."

"Not computers?"

She scrunched up her face. "Too much software, not enough hardware for my tastes."

His lips twitched.

"You all right?" she asked.

"I'm trying so hard not to make an inappropriate joke about hardware."

"Who says I wouldn't enjoy an inappropriate joke?"

"Well, maybe I'm trying to come across as cultured and non-pervy?" he suggested, leaning closer to her. He smelled so good, even under the clearly expensive cologne he was wearing, she detected a spicy, smoky scent that seemed to emanate off his skin.

"*Boring*," she told him with a smile, aware that he was staring at her mouth.

"Thank you, for sharing all that with me. Even though I probably don't deserve that trust," he said.

"I want you to know me," she admitted. "But it's scary, telling you things I haven't told anyone. Eventually, I want you to tell me about you."

He shrugged. "I'm an open book."

"Somehow, I don't think that's true." Watching his mouth, she thought back to their first kiss and wanted to feel that again so badly, the buzzing fire on the nerves. And why not? She leaned forward, twining her fingers carefully in his shirtfront to pull him closer. She pressed her lips to his, breathing him in. He moaned into her mouth and it made her shiver.

He tasted of her favorite beer, and even if he couldn't stand that flavor, she *loved it*. She slipped her tongue past his lips so she could reach more of it. He slid his hands into her hair with a reverence that made something deep inside her pulsate like a struck bell.

His right hand traced the lines of her arms reverently as she pulled her shirt over her head. His other hand slid up her ribs, never quite grasping her – just tempting her. His light, teasing touch could almost be considered cruel, if she wasn't enjoying it so much.

To pay him back, Eva dragged her fingertips up his thigh, but never put her hand near the developing bulge in his pants. He whimpered, rolling his hips toward her hand, only for her to dip that hand around his back and squeeze his firmly rounded cheek.

He laughed into her mouth. "All right, all right, I had that coming."

He carefully maneuvered them so she was lying back on her shirt to protect her skin from dock splinters. He'd thrown his leg over her hips, demonstrating some pretty impressive core strength as he sort of hovered instead of grinding down on her like an over-enthusiastic prom date. She tugged him down, wrapping her legs around his waist. He moaned, tipping his forehead against her as his hips thrust down. She almost bit his lip when that heavy, hot weight pressed *just so* against her.

Touching him wasn't enough anymore. She was a breath away from tearing those sensible clothes of his off, throwing them in the water and riding him until he went cross-eyed.

She was *aching* for him, and that was a scary thought, to want him so badly. She wasn't sure she'd wanted anything so badly since entering the human world. The last time she'd wanted something that badly, she'd upended her entire life.

Eva backed away from Alex and he followed, sitting up so his mouth followed hers. He was adorably dazed and unfocused, making her smile. "As much as I would like to go in the direction where this is going, I think we need to slow down."

He took a deep breath through his nose, gently wrapping her hair around his fingers as he nodded. "As much as I would like to argue with you, you're probably right. I mean, I'm *there* but I don't know if the rest of me would like the consequences of getting *there* too early. I don't want to rush it and ruin things. I don't want this to just be some casual, one-time thing. It's not just physical, for me. I *like* you, a lot of you. I would like to – oh, God, this sounds so after-school special, but I would like to date you. I would like–"

She kissed him again. It had been a long time since she'd wanted anything like that, but she thought maybe she wanted it, too. Even if she had no idea how to go about it.

"Well, when we finally get there together," she said, making him laugh. "I could always pull out the jewelry, make it part of the fun. You know, there's this story about Jillian and Bael in his treasure horde–"

He interrupted her with another kiss. "Nope, no, thank you. I don't want to hear it. I have to look her in the eye at work."

7

———

ALEX

ALEX FELT like he was about sixteen years old, facing down his prom date's father. But his metaphorical prom date's dad was about a hundred years older than him. So was his prom date, for that matter – older, even. Also, he never went to prom because he was technically home-schooled.

So really, the metaphor didn't work, but the feeling was still accurate.

Alex stood outside Jon's house, adjusting his collar – which seemed to be strangling him all of a sudden – and shifting the weight of his gift basket from one arm to the other. He'd been careful not to come by until Eva left for the day, which was quite the feat, considering the long hours both Alex *and* Eva kept.

Jon opened the door, a confused expression on his face that only got more intense when he saw the larder full of bribes, er, gifts Alex was bearing. "Um, Eva's not here."

"I know. I came by to see you," Alex said.

"Well, if you're trying to court me, I think Lia would tell you that ship has sailed," Jon said, chin pointing to the basket.

"No, this isn't a courting gift exactly. But as the closest thing Eva has to family, I thought it would help if I showed that I was serious about my intentions. I know I've screwed up, but I'm very interested in Eva. I really like her and I'm not in this for a casual fling. I know that some *magique* take the whole gift thing pretty seriously. And I don't know as much as I should about gnomes, so just in case, here you go."

He handed the laundry-hamper-sized basket to Jon, who worked not to buckle under the surprising weight. "Good grief, what's in this thing?"

"Sea stones shipped directly from your home waters in the Orkneys. An obscenely expensive Scotch. A sweater made from wool shipped from Edinburgh. Scotch tablet candy," he said, pointing out all of the goods Jessica had procured from League sources. "And a bagpipe."

Jon deadpanned. "What, they didn't have a haggis you could stick in here?"

"Haggis are more difficult to mail than you would expect," Alex replied.

"Well, at least you didn't mix us up with the Irish and gift me a shillelagh," Jon sighed, setting the basket aside. He extended his hand and in a formal tone, said, "Thank you for the gifts. And while I appreciate the gesture, if Eva ever found out about this, it would not be pretty. She's her own woman. She doesn't need my approval or disapproval for who she dates. If you want to date her, you need to give *her* gifts."

"I'm aware of that. And I have a plan in place," Alex said. "I just figured it couldn't hurt... unless she finds out about it."

"All right then, we're in agreement," Jon said. He seemed a little reluctant as he said, "You want to come in for a beer?"

"Thanks, but no, I've got some paperwork I've got to catch up on," Alex said. "I've um, lost track of the time I would normally spend after-hours keeping on top of that sort of thing."

"Because you've been spending it chasing after Eva, apologizing to Eva or just thinking about Eva?" Jon grinned at him. "Lia and I struggled with that a little, too, at first. Hell, so did Sonja and Will. Jillian says it's 'work-life balance' and we all need to get better at it. But when you have a good reason, it gets easier."

With that, Jon shut the door and Alex muttered to himself, "I'm in trouble."

———

ALEX DIDN'T EXPECT to encounter any problems on the short drive to Eva's, but he'd no sooner pulled out of Jon's driveway when he spotted a black truck on the side of the road. The same black truck with tinted windows he'd seen a few times in Eva's vicinity. A solidly built man with thick dark hair pulled back into a bun, was kneeling beside the front driver's side tire. He seemed to be *pretending* to fix the tire, but he didn't really seem to be *doing* anything. He had a toolbox out, but he wasn't holding any tools. The hubcap wasn't removed. Hell, the tire wasn't even flat.

The fact that he was parked within spitting distance of the turn to Eva's driveway put a sense of dread, cold and heavy, in Alex's gut. Was this guy trying to play on Eva's sympathies, to get her to stop and help him. Wasn't there a serial killer used to do that sort of thing? Never mind the fact that Alex himself had once needed Eva's help. He'd been sincere in his need... and he hadn't parked right outside of her house.

What if this guy tried to hurt Eva? Sure, she said she had superhuman strength, but what did that mean, really? Humans weren't that strong. And what if this guy was an equally strong *magie*? If Alex drove by and just hoped the guy had good intentions, how much danger would that mean to her?

No. It was simply unacceptable that Eva should be in danger, at risk, or even inconvenienced. The tremulous cold feeling in his belly wouldn't go away until he knew Eva was safe. Alex slowed his SUV to a crawl and parked it in front of the truck. He pasted on his best "League public forum where everybody complains" smile and got out.

"Hi, there!" Alex exclaimed. "Do you need some help?"

The man stood, several inches taller than even Alex's frame, and seemed to be fighting the urge to glower at him. His dark eyes

– they were *so* dark; Alex didn't think he saw a divide between the pupils and the iris – darted towards Eva's driveway in a way that made Alex distinctly uncomfortable. The man moved between Alex and the driveway. It was a territorial move, Alex thought, the sort of thing you saw on nature specials when a predator protected his kill.

"No, thank you," Man Bun grumbled. "It's nothing I can't handle."

"Oh, I'm happy to help. I'm Alex Lancaster, executive director of League operations in town. I'm a friend of the lady who lives just there." Alex nodded toward Eva's house. "A very close friend."

It was probably a dick move, flexing League muscle and making it clear that muscle extended to protecting Eva, but... yeah, Alex didn't have justification for it. His discomfort was skyrocketing and he just plain didn't like this whole situation. Even if the guy was just romantically interested in Eva, this was a weird way of going about it.

Man Bun didn't respond, merely frowned.

"What seems to be the problem?" Alex asked, peering down at the tire. It definitely seemed intact and inflated.

"I think it's off-balance," Man Bun rasped. "And there's no repair shop here in town."

"Oh, yeah, that happens all the time with these muddy roads," Alex said, leaning casually against the truck. He wished he had some sort of psychic gift like Cordelia's, so he could interpret the man's thoughts through touch. "You'd be better off taking it to the shop over in Hewitt or St. Sebastian."

"But I heard the lady who lives here works on engines," the guy protested.

"Yeah, engines on boats. Not tires on trucks," Alex noted. "And parking outside her house isn't the way to get her help. You need to move along."

The man's thin lip curled back away from sharp, white teeth. Dread curled in Alex's belly. Alex wasn't much for direct confrontation. In fact, he'd lost most of the fights he'd gotten into.

He was more of a negotiator. But his need to keep potential creeps away from Eva's doorstep outweighed any sense of self-preservation.

Maybe he could move fast enough to scoop that wrench out of the toolbox?

"I don't think I need to do anything I don't feel like doing," Man Bun said, smirking. "And you can't make me."

"You're right," Alex said. "I can't make you. But I'm not the one you need to worry about. I don't think you want to know what would happen to you if you tried to intrude on the lady's privacy."

"I can decide that for myself," Man Bun seethed, stepping forward, his shoulders hunched.

Alex raised his fists, only to hear the roar of a motorcycle behind him. It was a familiar sound, one of the loudest damn engines in the parish. He felt his shoulders give a little in relief. Back up had arrived in the form of a large bear with governmental powers.

"Alex?" Zed called. "You all right there?"

Alex nodded. "Yeah, this gentleman was just moving along."

Zed parked his bike while Alex continued to stare the man down.

"I don't have to go anywhere!" Man Bun barked, though he was eying Zed warily. Much more warily than he'd eyed Alex, which Alex tried not to resent. "What are you gonna do about it?"

"The way I see it, your tire's in good shape, so you should probably move along," Zed said, leaning against Alex's SUV. He smiled at Man Bun with a viciousness Alex had never seen from the usually gentle mayor. "I can wait all night, and I will. Because the woman in that house is one of mine. So is this guy."

Zed jerked a thumb towards Alex, and it was all he could do not to grin at Zed. He was sure Zed was only saying it to prevent retaliation against Alex, which would complicate Zed's job, but it was nice all the same.

Man Bun bit out an oath in a language Alex didn't understand. Zed's smile grew even wider. Man Bun seemed to be calculating his chances against Zed and decided the probability of an ass-whooping was pretty high. Alex tried not to be insulted that he didn't receive equal consideration, but Zed was Zed. And Alex was not. Man Bun slammed his tools into the back of his truck and jumped in the driver's side, flipping them both the bird as he sped off.

"So you gave Jon a basket full of rocks, wool and weird candy?" Zed asked, his mood brightening.

"It was a *sweater* – what is there a group text or something?" Alex demanded.

"Of course there is," Zed scoffed. "We'll add you."

"Please don't, I don't think I'm ready," Alex protested.

Zed shook his head. "No one is."

Alex nodded down the road, towards the dust cloud left by Man Bun's truck. "So what are we going to do about that asshole?"

"He could be a creep who sucks at taking no for an answer. He could be a real problem. Let's hope for creepy but prepare for problems." Zed jerked his shoulders. "I suppose Bael and I doing an overnight stake-out right here would be an invasion of Eva's privacy, huh?"

Alex thought about the key fob in his pocket that summoned a League version of a SWAT team. As much as he wanted to push the button to summon them, the prerequisites hadn't been met. Calling them willy-nilly could create some real problems in Mystic Bayou and in Alex's career. "Eva would probably think so at this point."

"Then I'm gonna leave it up to you two, to figure this out," Zed told him. "But he shows up to her house again? Invasion of privacy be damned. We don't take chances."

As Zed drove away, Alex pulled his SUV close to Eva's house. She came out of the door, a confused look on her face. "Did I just hear someone peeling off in a huff with a badly tuned motor? Also, is that Zed's bike parked down the road? I thought I heard it, too."

"Yeah," Alex said, grimacing. "Have you noticed a black truck around town, tinted windows? It might have showed up around town a few too many times."

Eva blew out a long breath through her nose. "There was this guy in the grocery store, a few weeks back. Spent way too much time reading a jock-itch medication box for it to be a legitimate purchase. But when I told him to fuck off, he fucked off, so I figured that was the end of it."

"Shark eyes?" Alex asked. "Man bun?"

"Yes!"

"And you didn't think to tell us?" Alex asked, working to keep his tone kind.

"Well, I thought it would sound a little silly," she said, throwing up her hands.

"I think we've learned that in this town, that sort of thing is never silly." Alex kissed her lightly. "And I just found him parked at the end of your driveway, pretending to need help with his truck."

"Oh, shit," she breathed.

"I thought you had super-senses."

"Well, it's not like bat sonar or anything." She shrugged. "He would have to move close or make noises for me to know he was there."

"I don't like it."

"There's not much I can do about you liking it or not." Her eyes suddenly narrowed. "Zed wanted to camp out in my yard, didn't he?"

"He used the word 'stake out' but I think it was because it sounded more serious," he said.

She snorted and seemed to think it over for a moment. "For right now, I think I have a handle on things, but I'll let you know if that changes."

"That's all I ask."

"So, you gave Jon a haggis?" she asked, ushering him through the front door.

"No, that was the one thing I *didn't* get him because the shipping was prohibitive! Stupid group text!" Alex groaned.

"No, I get it. Courtship gifts are a big deal in my culture, so I appreciate the effort." Eva nudged him down on her sturdy cream-colored sofa. It was so simple and comfortable, but so *her*. The care she had to take, to make sure it stayed clean with her occupational hazards, spoke of how much she cared about her home. "You know, if I was still living with my family, you would have been expected to present my father with an unusual jewel that was very difficult to find. If stealing it from a pissed off cave-dwelling *magie* was involved, even better."

"Sadly, my story involved a cranky personal assistant," he said. "But she is plenty scary. Oh, wait."

He dashed out to his SUV and pulled out the gift he'd wrapped for her. Well, Jessica had wrapped it for him, because he always used too much tape and made it look like a suspicious, potentially explosive package. After tearing off the paper, she reached the first layer. Given her penchant for novelty bandanas, he thought she would enjoy this part. Nestled in several unfolded bandanas printed with bananas and tiny pies and cupcakes, he'd placed a bottle, a can, and a package of cookies.

"What's this?" she asked, smiling but confused.

"This is as much information about Siobhan's banana cream pie recipe as I could sneak to you," he said. "I was afraid to ask her for the actual recipe because I heard she threatened a tourist with a lemon zester when he tried that a few weeks back. But, as her connection to expensive and difficult to find ingredients, I happen to know she uses the vanilla from Madagascar, this British brand of condensed milk and these Italian wafer cookies as the base of the crust. I thought it would help you duplicate it at home, and you wouldn't have to fake being stressed about work to get the banana cream pie."

"You are a very nice man." She made a face that he was pretty sure would normally be directed at adorable puppies, and then kissed him. He tried not to take the puppy thing personally if it got him kisses. "It's still so hard to believe you would do all this for me."

"Stop it," he told her. "Look, I've been through the wringer, romantically speaking. And when I find someone who interests me, who is *interested* in me, who wants to be with me, I do what I have to do to make my intentions clear before they move along."

"OK, you've said things like that before," she objected. "What does that even mean?"

He sighed, taking her fingers and twining them with his. "I was married before."

"All right." She nodded. "It wasn't to Cordelia, was it?"

"Well, no, not really, that was more of an unofficial teenager carnival marriage thing involving a carousel," Alex said.

She nodded, smirking. "Oh, one of those."

"It wasn't legally binding," he said. "But the marriage to my girlfriend from law school? Very legal and binding."

"Can we go back to the carnival thing for a second?" she asked. "What was it like, growing up like that?"

He shrugged and then slipped his arm around her shoulders. "I mean, in a lot of ways, it was every kid's dream. I could eat funnel cake every day of the week."

She grinned. "Which is also *my* dream."

"I saw so much of the country, more than any kid could dream of. I had friends, other kids whose families were traveling with us. I had adventures. I had a happy family. I mean, my parents *love* each other. I grew up knowing that."

"I'm sensing a 'but' coming," she said.

"There's no permanence to it. You never feel like you have a real home, like other kids." He made a gesture towards her house with its cozy rooms and comfortable furnishings. "I wanted to build that with someone. I thought I was building it with Lizzie. On paper, it should have worked. I thought we were *enough*, Lizzie and me. We were a lot alike, career-oriented, goal-oriented. We seemed to have this talent for getting along in life. And when we both received job offers in the same city, it just felt like we should get married. We'd been dating for two years. All of our friends were getting married. There was no reason *not* to get married. So, we had ourselves a sensible little ceremony followed by a reception in Lizzie's parents' church hall."

His parents hadn't been able to make it, he reminded himself, with more than a little bitterness. The carnival had a run of dates in Kansas.

"We rented an apartment in an area outside DC, amongst a bunch of other young urban professionals. We worked and came home and made salads for dinner every night, for God's sake. We couldn't have been more of a grown-up if we'd spent every night studying routine gutter maintenance and comparing term life policies," he said.

She giggled. "So not much about your life has changed, you incurable adult."

"I am who I am," he said, throwing up his hands. He was glad she could find the humor in this, that she wasn't hurt by his talking about his marriage. He wasn't telling her to put her off-balance or to let her know what he was used to. He just wanted her to *know* him, to know why he did the things he did sometimes – even if they were stupid. "I couldn't tell her about my work, of course. I'd been recruited before I'd even started law school, with the League paying my tuition and guaranteeing me an entry-level job when I needed one. I'd signed so many NDAs, I couldn't even tell her which part of town my office building was in. All she knew was that I worked for a government-adjacent organization, and I had to travel sometimes. Lizzie worked for a nice normal, human-owned firm that did patent law! How was I supposed to tell her that I went to work every day with people who could control the weather or turn into a lion if the copier pissed them off?"

She blinked at him. "I never considered how hard it would be to live with someone who didn't know this world existed. That must have been brutal."

"Especially when I came home with dragon damage to my pants," he said. "Also, did you know there are some breeds of dragon that spit acid when they're mad about interest rates?"

She shook her head, smiling gently. "I did not."

"Well, it's hell on linen, let me tell you." He shuddered. "Still, for a year or so, I thought we were happy. We saved for a house and had even put a big down payment on the perfect starter home, a place to raise children... and then Lizzie panicked, disappeared from work and drove to her parents' place three states away. She couldn't explain why she didn't want to be married to me anymore, only that I didn't make her happy. I didn't know how, really. And I never stopped to think about whether she made me happy. I just knew that most people got married when they went out into the world, and I thought we should do the same. Does that make me an asshole?"

She lifted a hand to push his hair back from his temple. "It makes you someone who wasn't entirely in touch with his feelings, or other people's feelings, not necessarily an asshole."

He sighed, leaning into her touch. Lizzie's leaving had been a blow. Years later, the rejection of it all still stung. She hadn't even returned his calls, only responding through counsel for their divorce proceedings. It just didn't work. Why hadn't it worked?

Alex had thought he'd done the right things, the responsible things. He thought he loved Lizzie, though he wondered now if he even knew what that meant. He liked her quite a bit, but he didn't feel that bone-deep "can't live without her" affection he'd expected to feel for the person he was going to spend the rest of his life with. Not like the feelings he was starting to develop towards Eva, in such a short amount of time – the absolute terror he'd felt over the possibility of not getting to be near her.

Maybe he'd only loved what Lizzie had represented – normalcy. She had grown up in the suburbs in a two-parent home, going to the same school for all twelve grades with the same kids. But despite the difference in their childhoods, they'd had so much in common – their interests, their goals, their work ethic. It should have worked, but somehow, it just didn't. Lizzie was a good woman with a kind heart... and she'd seen something in him that made her run. Something was missing in him – and in their relationship. Maybe deep down, what he'd really expected was for her to help him figure out the real world. Well, the "normal" world outside of the carnival. And that hadn't been fair to her.

They sat there quietly, holding each other as the sun set and left purple shadows creeping across the room. He felt hollowed out, though he wasn't sure whether it was abject dread he'd felt when he found Man Bun lurking outside of Eva's property or because of his lengthy confession. It was probably the latter. He didn't realize he was looking down until she lifted his chin gently with her strong, warm hands.

"Would you do it again?" she asked.

He shook his head emphatically. So she followed up with, "So you're not an asshole. I mean, my parents had more of a business arrangement than a marriage. They're good friends. They genuinely like and trust each other. But I can't ever remember them kissing in front of me or saying, 'I love you.' They were never the reason for the other getting up in the morning. They were in the partnership for what they could get out of it. But I guess it works for them because they're honest about it."

"Is that normal for gnomes?" he asked.

"Not really. But not all human marriages are alike, right?" she said, laughing lightly. Too lightly. "There are some gnome couples who are insanely in love with each other. Just not in my family."

"That's kind of sad. Growing up, not seeing love."

She jerked her shoulders. "You can't miss what you don't know."

"Well, missing what you do know still sucks, so I can't say it's any easier on this end of things," he told her, making her smile.

"I've had partners," she told him. "Capable, focused partners who knew what they were doing."

Alex raised his hands. "I'm happy for you, but I don't need exact details."

She snickered "But I've never been with someone I connected with emotionally. That's been nice. Feeling something for you, other than lust."

When his face fell, she leaned in, dragging the absolute tip of her tongue across his bottom lip. "But you should know that lust is definitely mixed in there, too."

He leaned across the couch and kissed her, pulling her close. Hell, he pulled her into his lap, enjoying the solid weight of her stretched across his thighs. He was very much looking forward to indulging that lust and all the other somethings, but it wasn't the right time. He was tired, but it was a good kind of tired, like when you were climbing out of bed for the first time after a long illness. He just wanted to sit here in the quiet dark with Eva and feel her in his arms, and him in hers.

It was an adjustment of his somewhat traditional norms, knowing that she had the strength here. But there was a sort of freedom in knowing that he wasn't in control, in knowing that he didn't have to be the strong one. She was making the choice to be there, and that was a balm to a lot of old wounds.

"Thank you, I appreciate that," he said. "So ends my TED talk on why I'm terrible with relationships."

"Is that what this is?" she asked. "A relationship?"

"It's going to be, if you'll have me," he said.

She tucked his head under her chin and hugged him tight. "I think you've made it clear I already have you."

8

EVA

EVA FORGOT to turn off the air circulating in her truck before she reached the Devil's Armpit. That had been a tactical error. She couldn't decide whether it would be a better idea to open a window to let that smell circulate out or keep the windows closed to keep more from circulating in.

She thought back to Alex's "trucking problem" and how the Devil's Armpit played into it. Alex wasn't entirely wrong, wondering if asking truckers to cross it on a regular basis was part of the issue. She definitely preferred her job, where questions of "how smelly is too smelly?" didn't come into play on a regular basis. Unless Jon had something spicy for lunch.

Still, it was a nice break to worry about someone else's problems for a little bit. It felt even better that she could be helping Alex solve a problem for the town, to remove a little bit of that burden from his shoulders. He definitely spent enough time trying to solve everybody else's problems.

As Eva was driving through the swampiest section of the Devil's Armpit, through a graveled section that always felt like she was rolling across a pathway of explosive marbles, she wondered why they had to bother with the road at all. Mystic Bayou was surrounded by *water*. Why couldn't the League just ship all of the stuff the town needed by boat? It would be more complicated, and the line from the Gulf, up the Mississippi, to the bayou wouldn't exactly be straight. And it would only be a temporary solution until the pressure on the League's resources eased. But… maybe it could work?

Eva was mulling over whether she should bother to bring this somewhat bizarre suggestion to Alex when she saw something stretched across the road in the distance, barely visible on the edges of her headlights. It was hard to see in the dark, but as she got closer, she could see it slithering across the lane like a snake made of metal spikes.

"What…?" Eva pressed her foot against the brake. The truck rolled to a stop ten feet short of the weird obstacle and she got out, unsure of what exactly she was looking at. It looked like the sort of thing police used to stop car chases in the movies. Why in the hell would it be all the way out here in the middle of nowhere? Had a state trooper let it drop out of their cruiser while they were passing? And why was it spray painted bright orange?

Eva stepped closer, wondering whether she should move the thing out of the way. Maybe it wasn't safe to touch it at all. She should definitely call Bael. She turned back toward her truck, frowning. It was times like this she wished she had one of those fancy satellite phones half the League people had. The breeze picked up and for a second, the Armpit's usual sulfurous stink seemed worse.

Eva moved to turn back to her truck and felt the gravel give a bit under her feet. It sprang back and suddenly, a spiked pole launched itself from under the road, a few bare inches from her bumper. If she'd stopped just a little closer to the chain, that pole would have bolted right through her engine block and disabled her truck entirely. If she'd run over the chain, her tires would have been taken out. Either way, her truck would have been out of commission, and she would be stuck out here in the dark.

"What in the billowing bowels of hell?" she gasped, scrambling back.

In the distance, she could hear a howl. It wasn't the mournful, moon-longing howl of a coyote. It was *angry,* and in its wake she could hear screaming. The layered cries of horror and anguish blended together in a tortured chorus that rang in her ears.

And Eva didn't know how she knew, but whatever this thing was, it was out to get *her.* She wasn't a victim of opportunity. This was hunting *her.* Those screams were meant to frighten *her.* And soon she would be screaming right along with them.

Another howl rang out, closer.

Yes, she had super-strength. And yes, she was harder to damage than most, so she might be able to withstand an attack from whatever was running at her.

But, seriously, fuck this.

Quickly, she picked her way back to the truck, careful to step on her previous footprints.

She jumped inside the truck and locked the doors. She could still hear the screams inside the truck, as if the tortured mouths were pressed right against her ears. Another howl, just behind her, bellowed out as she backed her truck away from the obstacles. In her rearview, she saw it, red eyes that glowed like the coals of the forges. The inky shape of its body moved so stealthily, she could barely make it out in the darkness, even with her eyes. But it was gaining speed, which she could tell by the size of its eyes in the rearview. What in the hell was that thing?

Eva floored the gas, whipping the truck around the spike chain and plunging into darkness. She drove the road by memory, concentrating on the awful eyes behind her and the road in front of her, foot by foot, terrified that she would come upon another booby trap. And somehow, the screams grew louder. It was like she could feel the pain of the damned, squeezing her chest and making it hard for her to breathe, much less concentrate on driving. She gasped, dragging the air deeply into her lungs. "Fuck you, you awful fucking thing. You are not going to kill me on some deserted road."

Gritting her teeth, she counted the mile markers one by one

until she reached the parish limits. At the first glimpse of Main Street, the screams inside her ears softened to a roar. The closer she came to the Parish Hall, the easier she could breathe. The eyes in her rearview faded until she could barely see them. She commanded her foot to draw back from the gas. The last thing she wanted to do was hit somebody in her panic.

What could she do now that she had made it to "home base"? She couldn't just go to her house, could she? That seemed ill-advised, to isolate herself. And she wasn't sure she would ever sleep again. What was the point of going home?

She saw the lights were on in Alex's trailer and, for a moment, the urge to park next to his SUV and run inside his place was overwhelming. She knew Alex probably couldn't protect her from whatever that thing was, but the idea of not being left alone with her fear was so tempting. It felt like a shelter in the storm. But she couldn't do that to him.

Alex was so fragile and human. She couldn't put him in danger just to make herself feel better. She wanted him protected from whatever this was. Preferably safe somewhere inside a secured League facility involving those bank vault doors.

Eva scanned the street, trying to find some alternative. She let out a little cry of relief when she saw Bael walking out of the pie shop with a carryout bag. She practically hockey-slid the truck into a rare free parking space. Bael stopped in his tracks, alarmed enough that she could see smoke rings billowing out of his nose – a clear warning she'd just about scared the dragon out of him. Literally. But when he recognized her truck, he dropped the carryout bag and ran for her driver's side door. "Eva? You OK?"

Staring through the glass, she wondered, what was she supposed to say? Her thoughts were all jumbled up, leaving her foggy and tired. Frowning, Bael opened the unlocked truck door, gently reached past her, and turned the key in the ignition.

"Eva, I think you might be going into shock. I need you to take some breaths for me, all right?" he told her, his voice so soft and kind, it practically brought tears to her eyes. "Do you want me to call Jon? Er, Alex? Anyone?"

She swallowed thickly. "I don't want to sound paranoid, but I think someone just tried to set a trap for me. Out in the Devil's Armpit."

To her surprise, Bael simply nodded and smiled at her. "OK, then, we can handle that. I'll call Jillian. You hungry?"

————

IT WAS A LITTLE ALARMING, how easily they accepted her story. There were no scoffing minimizations or assurances. She was led to a League trailer at the back of complex, Bael's hands under her elbows just in case her knees gave out. There were no bank vault doors, but she was clearly in some sort of interrogation room with reinforced cement block walls, two-way mirrors, metal tables with big loops in the middle for securing prisoners. Bael was gentle with her, treating her like a survivor instead of a suspect, which helped calm her. He fetched her hot, sweet tea and a slice of bourbon meringue pie that Siobhan insisted was just the thing to settle her nerves.

While they waited for Jillian, she dug her fork through the crispy meringue shell to the downy sweetness. Her hands shook slightly before she could lift the fork to her mouth. Bael nudged the tea towards her.

"It's just the adrenaline draining out of your system," he assured her. "Happens to everybody when they're in life-or-death situations."

She scooped her fork down and somehow managed to get the perfect balance of meringue and brown, whiskey-tinged filling. She swallowed the pie and felt a peaceful sort of warmth, not quite calm, but certainly better than she'd felt before. She drank the sweet tea and breathed deeply. She was safe. Whatever had been chasing her could not bust through these walls.

Her ears perked at the thump of heavy footsteps thundering down the hallway.

And she definitely wasn't alone.

"Eva!" Zed yelled as Jon bumped against him, practically knocking him out of the way to get in the door first. "Ow! Dammit, Jon!"

Jillian rolled her eyes fondly as she walked around their struggling mass of limbs to get to Eva first. Eva practically melted against her friend as Jillian squeezed her tight. "Hey, sweetie. I'm glad you called."

Bael kissed his wife. "Is the baby with Clarissa and Mel?"

Jillian nodded and began setting out recorders, notebooks, and various interview tools.

"What are you doing here?" Eva asked as Jon pulled her from the chair and hugged her so hard Eva's breathing was actually affected. That was impressive.

"He's your emergency contact," Zed informed her, pulling Eva from Jon's grip and hugging her. "Bael made it sound like an emergency."

"It says a lot about what y'all have been through, that you know what to do in this situation," she sighed.

"Well, we've finally learned our lesson. People we love start experiencing weird stuff, we handle it officially and quickly. Otherwise, chaos and bullshit ensue." Zed jerked his shoulders and slid into the seat next to Eva. "You OK, *cher*?"

"I'm just... tired and unsure of whether I should be making such a big deal over this, but it was so awful. The screams, I could hear them in my head. And it felt so personal. This thing was out to get *me*, not just whoever rolled by those spikes. Me."

"Wait, screams and spikes?" Bael exclaimed. "Eva, why don't you take us back to the beginning. I think we're gonna need all the details."

Outside, Eva heard car wheels rolling over the gravel. When she startled, Zed patted her hand. "It's all right, *cher*. We've got all night, or until the *bebe* burns all of Mel's knitting supplies. Which personally, I am rooting for. Because I'm not a fully matured man, yet, and Mel insists on kissing my *maman* in front of me."

"But we still love you," Jillian assured him. "Besides, Mel has a fireproof yarn safe after last time."

"Dammit," Zed grumbled.

"Eva!" Alex yelled from the front door of the trailer.

The part of Eva that had turned ice cold when she'd heard those horrible screams finally grew warm again. "Is that Alex?"

"We thought we should call him," Bael said. "Being the head of League operations and all. He was at a meeting in New Orleans. Probably did ninety to get back here so fast."

Jillian lifted her brow. And Bael added, "Which I will not mention, despite it being a clear violation of state and local traffic laws."

Jon and Zed snickered. Bael glared at them. "Shut it."

Alex burst into the room, and like something out of an old-fashioned movie, pulled Eva into his arms and kissed her until she was practically bent backward.

Jon muttered, "I am standing *right here*."

Alex pulled away, clutching her face in his palms and looking her over for damage. "Are you all right? You're not hurt?"

"I'm fine. I'm just happy to see you," she assured him as he kissed her all over again.

"Oh, come on now," Zed sighed.

"See?" Jon huffed. Zed crossed his arms over his chest, grimacing.

Behind Alex's back, Eva made a hand motion that translated to "shut it, both of you."

"If you could un-attach your face from Eva's, we're trying to take her statement," Bael said dryly. After a few more kisses, Bael grumbled, "OK, it's gonna be hard taking an official report with your tongue in her mouth."

Alex pulled away again, clearing his throat. "Sorry."

"Just so you know, Jon's not alone. In my mayoral capacity, I'm trying really hard not to punch you in the face right now, so—" Zed turned Eva gently, licked his palm and pressed it to her forehead. "You are hereby adopted as my sister."

"Well, that's not fair. Just because selkies don't have a forehead ritual, I'm just as much her unofficial sibling as you are!" Jon protested.

"It's hardly an actual ritual," Jillian said to Eva. "Zed seems to believe that if he licks something, that makes it his." Then she shrugged. "He does the same thing with the last cookie in a box."

"And once, an entire blackberry cobbler," Bael added. "His *maman* was pissed."

Eva swallowed thickly. She couldn't speak for the bliss of it, of not being alone in the world, having people she could run to when things got difficult. It was exhausting, having her emotions swinging so wildly back and forth all night. She just wrapped her arms around Zed and then pulled Jon into their hug. She tucked her face into Jon's neck and breathed in the scent of her family before releasing them.

"Multiple adopted sisters!" Zed raised his arms in triumph. "I have so many subtle threats to make to their boyfriends!"

"None of your threats are subtle," Bael told him. "But congratulations to you both."

Eva nodded while blinking furiously. Zed glowered at Alex, and then grinned with evil intent.

"I knew I presented bribes to the wrong guy," Alex muttered.

"I hate to interrupt this beautiful moment," Jillian said, smiling fondly at them. "But I believe we were about to talk about the screaming and the spikes?"

Alex's eyes went wide. "I'm sorry, what?"

Eva glanced at Alex, imagining his reactions to the story she was going to tell. "Could you ask Siobhan to send over more whiskey to go with my pie? Maybe some for Alex, too."

———

Eva had to hand it to her friends; they certainly asked questions like seasoned investigators. She was absolutely exhausted after spending the better part of two hours detailing everything she saw, heard, smelled, and felt. And they *believed* her. They just accepted this insane story about what seemed to be an otherworldly dog chasing her through the Devil's Armpit. They were *worried* about her and offered her multiple options of places to stay so she wouldn't be left alone in her house overnight. And Alex—sweet Alex—gave her a deep sense of comfort that she hadn't expected to feel. It wasn't a familiar sensation to her, but she could certainly get used to it.

Eventually, Alex interrupted Jon and Zed's bickering to tell them that Eva would stay with him at his trailer. Then there was a whole argument over whether Alex could actually protect Eva if, as Zed put it, "shit went down."

Alex responded. "I have a SWAT team on call at the touch of a button. Do *you* have a SWAT team on call at the touch of a button?"

"No." Zed pouted. "That is pretty cool."

While Eva was still *extremely* concerned about whatever the hell saw fit to set a booby trap in the road for her, there was a feeling of peace settling over her as Alex walked her the short distance to his home. People *cared* for her here. People were arguing over the privilege of taking her into their homes to keep her safe. She never thought she would be in that position. And Zed? Her family had never made her feel as accepted as Zed did when he rubbed his saliva on her forehead.

Which was a *super* weird thing to be grateful for.

Fortunately, she had an overnight bag packed in her truck with everything she needed.

"I always have one ready," she explained. "I do not like driving home from a job site in stained, soiled clothes."

"I do the same thing," Alex told her. "With my job, you never know when you're going to be stuck somewhere unexpectedly. I mentioned the dragon acid thing. But sometimes, you just don't want to be stranded in Saskatchewan without clean underwear."

"I will take your word for it," she replied as he unlocked the door.

His trailer was new and nice, but so plain. She spotted a few framed photos of people she assumed were his family members around the living room, but it was sort of sad how little of his personality she saw in the place.

"I'll take the couch," he told her quickly. "I don't want you thinking I'm taking advantage of your emergency to get you into bed."

She pursed her lip. "What if I would be OK with that?"

He shook his head. "Cute, but you've been through a lot tonight. You're exhausted and I don't want to take advantage of you."

"Is it an issue of not wanting to have sex with me or you thinking *I* don't want to have sex with you?" she asked.

"Oh, hell, no, I really, really want to have sex with you, a lot of times," he insisted, then cleared his throat. "That sounded less weird in my head."

She kissed him soundly. "I really, really want to have sex with you, too."

Then she picked him up and slung him over her shoulder, walking him down the hall towards what she assumed what his bedroom. She set him on his feet, realizing that she may have just gone too far. He might not appreciate being lifted and toted around like a swooning Regency heroine. Also, she could have hurt him.

Oh, no. How had it never occurred to her that she'd never been with a human before? Those aforementioned enthusiastic lovers of her past were all other *magique*, all much sturdier creatures. But Eva had to be careful with Alex. He was capable in a lot of ways, but he was fragile compared to her other lovers. But it was probably time for something softer for her. When he reached up to touch her face, it was so gentle she had to focus to feel it. It was making her slow down, making her connect with her body, not lose herself in how she felt alone. She didn't like to think of herself as a selfish lover... just determined to get what she needed. Too many times she'd been on the receiving end of a man's own "determination" and was left unsatisfied. If she worked to make sure she got there first, who could blame her?

OK, maybe it had made her a little selfish over time.

"Is everything all right?" he asked. "You seem sort of... frozen?"

"I could hurt you," she whispered. "Like, if I get distracted, too lost in the moment, I could put one hand down too hard on your shoulder and dislocate it."

She realized how panicked she sounded and cleared her throat. He slipped his hands over her cheeks and brought her eyes down to meet his. "OK, well, try not to do that?"

"Sure, like it's that simple," she snorted.

"I trust you," he told her, reaching for the button of her jeans. "If you start getting overwhelmed, let me know and we'll stop."

Thinking it over, she realized his plan was better than the idea of going to bed, untouched, with this awful, empty longing inside of her. She nodded and he waited until she reached for his clothes to push her jeans down her thighs. He knelt in front of her, kissing her stomach while he eased her cotton panties down. She reached back and took off her own bra, because she'd never met a man who could handle a five-hook enclosure without getting frustrated. She twined her fingers through his hair and crawled backwards on the bed.

All she could think as he crawled up her body was that he smelled *so good*, like walking through the cologne department at a fancy store. But she would never tell him so, because "You smell expensive" probably wasn't the compliment she wanted to deliver at that moment. He pressed light little kisses along her ribs before rolling them, so she was on top.

This was new for her. He was treating her like *she* was delicate and while she wasn't, there was a concern there that she found touching. And then he bit down on her nipple with a little less gentleness and she yelped, instinctively grinding her hips down.

Eva froze, worried that she might have pressed down a little too hard, but Alex's face was blissful as he paid equal attention to both breasts. She'd had all these good intentions, to go slow, to use finesse, but he was hard and hot against her − right *there*, and she was so wet that it was nothing to swerve her hips and ease him into her.

He gasped, gripping at her shoulders and groaning as she stretched to take him in.

She wriggled her eyebrows and smiled down at him.

"Just a minute," he whimpered. But she couldn't help it, her hips practically canted on their own as he bumped against that sweet little patch of nerves inside of her. He made a strangled noise, half-way between a moan and a shout. "It's been a while!"

"Sorry," she giggled, even though she was anything but. She wasn't sorry, she was *glorious*, and she wanted to take him right along with her. He pulled her close, breathing into her throat as he tried to relax. He was holding onto her as if she was the only thing anchoring him to the earth, and that was a pretty powerful thing.

Suddenly, Alex nodded frantically and arched his hips up into her. She moved slowly, not just to protect him but because she didn't want this feeling to end so quickly. She was already so tight, a terrible pressure building in her, and he was just so sweet underneath her.

It was a *dilemma*.

But she was already halfway to that plunge, focusing on gripping the metal brace that connected the slats of his headboard. A particularly powerful spasm rippled through her and she screamed, pulling at the brace. She felt it give under her hand, but she couldn't seem to stop herself as her back arched. She shouted and the brace came loose with a splintering groan. She looked at the twisted metal bar in her hand with horror.

Alex didn't seem disturbed at all, eyes glazed over as he pulled her down for a fierce kiss.

"It's fine," he insisted. "I don't think it's holding the bed together or anything. I can get another one if it is. Just keep going."

She wanted to protest. This could have been one of his limbs! She could have hurt him! But then he started rolling his hips again, hitting that spot inside her that made her nerves sing, and the metal clanged to the floor, forgotten. She joined him in that dance, riding out the pleasure that was still coursing through her veins. Alex turned them, rolling on top of her and sliding down her body, tracing the lines of her bones with his tongue.

As he paused between her thighs and grinned up at her, she gripped the two remaining braces on the headboard. He was going to need a stronger bed.

———

HOURS LATER, they stretched diagonally across the mattress, watching the light drag itself over her windows, as if the sun was just as exhausted as they were.

Alex's sleepy voice startled her from the cat nap she was about to slip into. "Can I ask you something?"

Eva rolled and tucked her face against his shoulder. "Yes, I am OK with that thing you did with your knuckle, but I understand if it's a 'special occasions only' move."

He burst out laughing. "No, that's just one of the many moves I plan to apply to you over time. It's just, I didn't want to say anything in front of everybody else because it involved stuff you've told me in private. But you mentioned that you and your family aren't on good terms, that you don't want them to find you. Do you think it's possible they're trying to find you? Maybe the Man Bun or whatever it was that chased you through the swamp was trying to get you and take you back?"

She hadn't wanted to consider it, but that had been lurking at the back of her mind since she'd heard the screams in the Devil's Armpit.

"Why are your parents looking for you so hard?" he asked, shaking his head. "Is it just the loss of reputation or is there something else? Several hundred years seems like a really long time to hold on to something like that. Even for pissed-off *magique*."

Eva sighed. It had been a thing to behold. Of course, it had just looked like an ordinary blue stone before her Aunt Lara cut it. Lara Orebender looked at the stone and cut away everything unnecessary until all that was left was a drop the size of a pigeon's egg, clarity so profound that when Eva turned it in her hand, she swore she could see it swirl like the sea water for which it was named.

She took his hand in hers. "There was this stone that my family was holding onto, the Ocean's Eye. My cousin found it in a rich vein in the southeast, had to fight a particularly nasty scorpion shifter to get it. It put his name in the family archives in the special gold ink. My family knew they wanted to wait until they could use it for something special, something that would make *our* name even greater. And then we got a commission from the League, a gift for some sea-bound emissary they were trying to woo. To prove that the Orebender name was unmatched, the youngest and least experienced among them would create this masterpiece – namely, me. Also, I could do link work my older relatives could only dream of."

The sketch was still in the bottom of her iron casket, all swirling silver waves and beveled aquamarines to bring out the bluer depths of the Ocean's Eye. She lost count of how many drafts she'd gone through before her mother was finally satisfied with the design. The links of the chain would be so fine, it would have lain across the wearer's throat like a lover's caress. Unfortunately, it was never completed.

"It was going to be this collar necklace made from pearls and aquamarines set in silver, surrounding the Ocean's Eye. It would have frothed at her throat like glittering sea foam. But I took it," she whispered. "I saw the stone, laying there in the strongbox in the workshop, and I thought about the price it would fetch in the human world, what it would mean to me, versus some sea nymph who would only take it out on official occasions. And I tucked it into my casket and ran."

It was like choking on sand, saying those words. Taking the stone had been her shame for a long time, Eva's burden to carry – the knowledge that she'd betrayed her whole family and everything they stood for, just to free herself. But he didn't pull away from her, he didn't call her a thief or leave the bed. Mostly, he just looked confused as to why *she* was so upset.

"So you took a jewel? Doesn't your family have a bunch of jewels?" he said, shrugging. "Can't you just trade them one?"

She blinked at him for a long time and then she kissed him. For just a minute, she felt a little bit of relief that she'd shared this darkest part of her story. And he hadn't rejected her. That was such a gift. "It was more about the fact that I made them look bad – to the League, to other families that work in jewelry, to other *magique* families. Professionally, it's just not acceptable to leave a commission unfilled after promises have been made. It was the first time it had happened with the Orebenders, and I'm sure that it hasn't happened since."

He asked, "So are they going to hurt you if they find you?"

There was a long pause as Eva searched inside of herself for an answer.

"The fact that you're not answering me is scary," he told her.

"I don't know," she said. "They're probably still angry with me. They believe I should be using my skills to further the family name."

He pulled her to his chest and kissed her forehead. "Well, that explains a lot. I just don't understand why you wouldn't just tell us this in the first place. It might have helped us."

"I was ashamed! I stole from my family!" Her voice cracked and she inhaled sharply. She'd never cried over this, not in all of her years. She didn't deserve to feel sorry for herself. But somehow, telling Alex had cracked that dam inside her, and she could feel the tears slipping between her cheek and his skin.

He rocked her gently, kissing her face over and over. "Trust me, there are plenty of people in town who have done equally desperate things to get out of bad situations. You know what Cordelia went through."

She nodded. He wiped at her cheeks with his thumbs. "I knew I had to get out of there, and that gemstone was my ticket to another life, a place where I could find some sort of fulfillment, instead of joyless... nothing. That was part of what sent me running, the idea that I would never enjoy my life, that what I wanted or needed, didn't have any value in comparison to living up to my name. I was just going to *endure* my life. For the rest of my days, I would be crawling up a staircase that went on forever, taking the same turns over and over, until I hated myself and resented everybody around me. And the thought of that, it just broke me, Alex. Leaving was the only way to save myself.

He wrapped his arms around her, and she felt her whole body tremble against him. She clenched her jaw and forced herself to settle so she could add, "Anyway, we need to update Zed and Bael and Jillian, so they know what we're dealing with. If you'd rather tell them yourself, I would understand. I don't want to put you in a bad position, but they need as much information as you can give them."

Eva groaned and pressed her face against his shoulder.

"They're going to understand," he promised. "They love you."

"OK," she whispered. "Thank you."

"Anytime," he said. "Seriously, any time you wanted to do any of that, I am available."

"Will you do the knuckle thing?" she asked, sniffling.

"Even if it kills me," he swore. "I'll die happy."

9

———

ALEX

HE WASN'T sure how he'd ended up moving into Eva's snug little house on the bayou. He drove her home the morning after she was chased through the Devil's Armpit, and he just failed to leave. It felt like his stuff slowly migrated into the house over the next week or so. His clothes had their own space in her closet. His shampoo was lined up next to her bottles in the shower. She took to keeping Anjou pears in the blue glass bowl on the counter because she knew he favored them.

It felt nice, knowing she was making room in her home for him. He worried that he'd moved too fast, that he would fall into the same trap that caught him with Lizzie – mistaking the motions of daily living with real happiness. But there was a depth to his joy in the little everyday things they did together – shopping for groceries, doing the dishes, sitting outside on the dock drinking Eva's formidable beer – that made his life with Lizzie look hollow in comparison. He would never say that out loud. It sounded like the reflections of a dick.

Avoiding "Reflections of a Dick" as the subtitle of his autobiography seemed like a good way to live his life.

It got to the point that it barely looked like he lived in his trailer... not that it did before. He just didn't want to leave her. He liked coming home to her at the end of the day. Every once in a while, he tried to make her dinner... but there was a fire. And that was how he learned that Eva was basically fireproof. She'd reached for the flaming pan without hesitation, tossing it into the empty sink and smothering the flames with a lid. She didn't even flinch when her sleeve caught fire. Alex had shrieked in a comic fashion and run for the first aid kit, but she didn't have a mark on her. It turned out it was a perk of gnome-dom. Being impervious to flames made them that much better at their jobs.

So now, he was trusted with chopping and stirring until he proved he could use a stove without incident.

Tonight, Eva was over at Ingrid's setting up some sort of irrigation system for some "struggling saplings" Ingrid was in a panic over, and he was content to lie on the couch and read paperwork. The only thing missing was a cat purring at his side. He wondered if he and Eva could get a cat. But so many pets were incompatible with *magique* because of their wilder natures. He didn't want to suggest anything that would make Eva feel bad.

Alex couldn't believe he was laying here, considering whether it would be ok to ask his... special lady partner who he happened to live with whether she would consider adopting a cat. This was definitely not where he saw his life going even six months ago. He sort of loved it.

Having slogged through League paperwork for a few hours when he got home, he was slowly catching up on some of the work that he'd missed now that he had other things to occupy his time. The only real pressing (and frustrating) problem still facing him was the trucking contract. While they weren't using magic as Jillian had suggested, according to Alex's sources, the trucking companies had indeed been in contact behind his back, mutually agreeing to hold off on signing until Alex agreed to a rate even higher than the League's generous terms. It seemed counter-intuitive to him, to work together so only one company could get the benefit. He supposed it was like playing the lottery, each of them hoping to be the lucky winner.

Still, he wasn't playing games, and this whole thing was becoming a problem. He had *never* failed to meet a goal his boss, Mr. Messina, set. Messina was not impressed with his lack of progress, and he mentioned in their last video call that maybe Alex was becoming too personally involved in the community to continue to be effective in Mystic Bayou. His career was about to be tanked by freaking shipping issues.

The alarm reminding him to call his parents sounded. He picked up his phone and stared at it. He could call his mother again and put her through the paces of trying to connect him to his family, to let her do all of the work, while his father avoided him. He thought about Eva and what her parents put her through and there was an uncomfortable parallel. Eva had been expected to do work she hated with no reward other than more work for her family. It seemed so massively unfair of Alex, to put all of that work on his mother's shoulders while his father skated by without consequences.

Breathing deeply, Alex scrolled through his contacts and tapped his father's number. His dad owned the last operating flip phone in the United States. The man couldn't even receive texts on it. But it worked, so Elliott insisted that it was still a vital piece of technology.

His dad picked up on the fourth ring. In the background, Alex could hear kids laugh-screaming, a sound he knew would turn to over-sugared tears within the hour. He could almost smell the heavy sweetness of frying oil and burning sugar.

"Hello? Who is this?" his dad barked. "I don't have all day!"

Alex rolled his eyes. It wouldn't surprise him if the screen on the flip phone no longer showed Elliott callers' numbers. It also wouldn't surprise him if his father no longer recognized Alex's phone number. Either way, this was not an auspicious beginning.

"It's Alex, Dad."

There was an awkward pause on the other end of the line, as if Elliott was trying to remember whether his son's name was, in fact, Alex.

"Alex? Why didn't you just call your mom?" he asked, shouting over the tinkling music of the Swirl-A-Nator as it roared to life.

"Because I've called Mom every week for months and you've always been too busy to talk so I thought it would be better to just call you," Alex replied.

"Why would you call if you knew I was busy?" Elliott demanded.

"Because no one is that busy, Dad," Alex shot back. "I run an entire town for an actual shadow government and *I'm* not that busy."

His father grumbled bitterly, "Yeah, well, you haven't been around in a long time. You don't know how bad things have gotten around here in the last few years."

"So retire!" Alex exclaimed. "You're sixty-seven years old. Mom says you have more than enough savings. Besides, if things got tight, you know I would help. Stop twisting yourself in knots trying to keep that place alive!"

Alex gritted his teeth. Only a few minutes into the conversation and he was already losing his temper. This wasn't the way to get through to his father. And it certainly wasn't the way to get his father to talk to him *more often*. Now that he thought about it, his father wasn't talking at all.

"It's not just this place," Elliott spat. "It's everything else, too."

There was a long pause.

"Dad?"

"I don't know what you want from me, son," Elliott said. "Your kind of life? I don't even understand it. I can't imagine spending the rest of my years being tied down to one place."

"You wanted that for me!" Alex cried. "You told me to go to law school, get an education, a 'normal' career. You said you didn't want me to follow you into your life!"

"I wanted *more* for you! Every father wants more for their son! But I didn't know how it would feel, watching you move so far away from the way you grew up, the way *I* grew up," Elliott huffed. "I feel like I don't even know you anymore."

"Well, you might if you actually picked up the phone instead of letting Mom do it. Then you'd find I haven't changed that much."

"I need to go, Alex," Elliott said quickly. "Next time, just call your mom. You know she looks forward to your calls. Don't take that from her."

"Fine." Alex closed the call, and it took all of his patience, honed from years of meetings with some of the most passive-aggressive creatures on the planet, to prevent Alex from throwing his phone at the wall. They'd only spoken for four-and-a-half minutes. How was he able to screw up a conversation with his father *that* fast?

Elliott said he didn't know what Alex wanted from him. The problem was that he didn't know what he wanted from his father, either. He didn't *need* his father to be proud of him. He knew that. He was a grown-ass man. But dammit, would it really be so hard? Was his life really so awful and disappointing that his father couldn't bear to come visit him? That his dad couldn't even bear to get through a five-minute conversation? Why was this so damned difficult?

Outside the house, he heard the crunch of tires on gravel. He sat up, looking out the window to see a black SUV coming up the driveway. Eva hadn't agreed to let him install a network of wireless cameras around her house, what the League security office called the "Peace of Mind Web" package. She'd made this face when he brought it up, like she couldn't imagine anything worse. And since it was *her* house, he'd dropped it. He realized that years on the run probably didn't make for a comfortable mindset *vis-à-vis* having your every move tracked. And he wanted her to be comfortable in her own home, especially when she'd made him so comfortable.

Zed and Bael came ambling out of the car. Jon and Will followed. They were carrying cases of beer and grocery bags.

"Oh, no," he whispered. Eva had told him about this. This 'spontaneous' social gathering thing that her friends did where they just showed up with snacks and drinks at the unsuspecting host's house. He never even had *planned* social gatherings at his house. Even the card games he joined with his coworkers were held outside in the "quad" between the trailers. And he only went to those on occasion because he didn't want to offend Ivy Portenoy and her death-tickle fingers.

He stood, eyes scanning the room for anything that could prove embarrassing – discarded underwear, fast food cartons, important financial paperwork – but to his surprise, he and Eva kept a pretty tidy house. So this was what it was like, being a grown-up with a company-ready home. He'd had that with Lizzie, he supposed, but they'd never had *friends* over. The occasional polite gathering of neighbors and Lizzie's coworkers, but never people he wanted to get close to, people he wanted to share his life with. Alex fluffed the throw pillows on the sofa and walked over to the door.

"Hey there, Al," Zed said, walking in and handing Alex a case of the lager he favored. "The girls sent us over, thought you might need some company with Eva over at Ingrid's."

"We invited Leonard and Rob, but they thought it might be kind of weird for you? Hanging out with your subordinates on your first try," Will said.

"I don't call them my subordinates!" Alex exclaimed, before adding, "To their faces."

Alex noted that Brendan didn't join them, either, but Alex didn't take that personally. It was very unlikely that the two of them were ever going to be close friends. There was too much history with Cordelia. Besides, it was a lot to have these four people in his living room. These four people that Eva loved and would want him to welcome into her home, he reminded himself.

"Come on in," he said, motioning awkwardly towards the living room. I'll get some bowls for the chips.

"We brought guacamole, too!" Jon called. "Lia made it especially for you."

"Well, that was nice of her," Alex said, again, awkwardly. When he returned from the kitchen, the guys had made themselves comfortable, as if they spent all of their time lounging around his living room. But no one was talking. He sat down, choosing a spot next to Bael on the couch. Bael was grinning at him.

Alex cleared his throat. "What?"

"It's just interesting, is all. We all love Eva, and we were curious as to what sort of person she'd end up with," Bael said. "We knew she wouldn't be alone for long. And it's *you!* You've been sort of dancing around the edge of our circle for a while, and I don't know, it's like playing the friendship lottery, sometimes, when your friends date."

Zed stared at Bael. "Did that come out the way it sounded in your head?"

"Did you expect Leonard to end up in our group?" Bael retorted, making Zed shrug.

Alex tried to focus on the nice things Bael said. "Well, of course, she wasn't going to be alone for long. Eva's smart and kind and funny. She doesn't just fix boats and bikes and trucks, you know? I dropped the toaster the other day and this spring popped out and it wouldn't toast anymore. And she did something with a screwdriver and it worked again. I don't understand it. I would have just gotten a new toaster, but she fixed it and it toasts even better now."

The guys were staring at him, smirking. And he was pretty sure Zed was making anime heart eyes.

"And she has super-powers," Alex added, feeling lame. "Which is surprisingly sexy."

"So you like the fact that she could basically snap you in half?" Jon said, raising a brow.

"I mean, it's not *why* I like being with her, but it's cool that my girlfriend has super-powers. And when she's holding herself back to avoid hurting me, that's... flattering?"

"I don't know if I'm comfortable talking about my friend this way," Jon said, clearly regretting the turn of this conversation.

"What he said." Zed pointed at Jon, his demeanor decidedly heart-eye-less.

"But we talk about our sex lives all the time," Bael said, shrugging, but he was smirking at Zed. Alex got the feeling Bael was leaning into the topic to mess with Zed, not Alex.

"But when we talk about our... various lady partner people, it's in clearly respectful terms," said Zed. "And with nowhere near the graphic detail that the ladies get into."

"Wait, Dani tells you what they say about *us?*" Bael asked, turning to Zed. "Well, what do they say?"

Zed shrugged noncommittally and sipped his beer, now clearly messing with Bael in a retaliatory fashion. "Nothing you should worry about. Really. I'm sure it's fine."

"I know what you're doing," Bael told him. "And given the amount of sleep I'm getting lately, it's just mean."

"Is this what you usually talk about when you get together?" Alex asked Will. "Sex problems and gossip?"

"No, it's usually one of us having an emotional crisis. Sex problems and gossip are actually pretty refreshing," Will replied.

"We're not having sex problems!" Alex cried.

"We can talk about my daughter and her fire-teething problems," Bael suggested.

Alex's lips pulled back in a fearful expression. "Fire-teething?"

Bael pursed his lips. "It's like regular teething, but with more fire."

"Yes, yes, let's talk about that," Alex insisted. "I'll get more beer."

"But we all have beers," Jon protested.

"We need more!" Alex called from the kitchen.

By the time he came back, they were talking about Bael's new industrially fireproofed living room furniture and Zed's new cell phone, which could withstand accidental lightning blasts from Dani's hands. Will was planning an informational clinic on *magique* pregnancies because the town was about to have a baby boom. Jon was thinking about adding on to the boat shop now that he and Eva were working at top speed.

Now that they weren't actively giving him shit, Alex could enjoy the conversation. It sort of ebbed and flowed from topic to topic, but it was easy to follow. This was familiar. It reminded Alex a little bit of when the guys would get together after closing up the carnival, packing everything up when it was too late to safely move along to their next stop, and just *sitting*. There was time to relax, even if just for a few hours, and enjoy the fact that there was nothing to run off to, nothing to concentrate on except just being together.

Alex wasn't in charge of much beyond pouring sawdust on puke when he was a kid, but he'd put in an honest day's work. Of course, he couldn't *legally* drink the beer when he sat around with the others, so when he was able to sneak a few sips, it tasted like the sweetest stuff on Earth.

He didn't contribute much to the conversation. He thought maybe that wasn't the point of them being there. Eva hadn't wanted him to be alone, he realized. She thought he might be lonely or even in danger, so she'd sent her friends to keep him company.

He was pretty sure he was in love with that woman.

The thought made his beer bottle still half-way to his lips.

Oh, God. He loved Eva. He was hopelessly, stupidly in love with Eva. He loved her brains and her hands and her beautiful face. He loved the way she could create something absolutely stunning out of bits of metal and stone, but preferred fitting gears together to make something useful. Her loved her laugh and the way she nudged him through problems. He loved the way she'd made a home with him and didn't let him work himself into the ground. He hadn't really had a life in Mystic Bayou before her. He'd existed, but he hadn't lived.

Holy hell.

Of course, he'd known that he definitely felt more for her than *like,* that somewhere along the line, he'd fallen in love with her – this insanely attractive and intelligent woman who fixed small appliances when he broke them.

How was he going to tell her?

He definitely shouldn't bring up the toaster. That was *not* the sort of romantic overture women dreamed of.

"You OK, Al?" Zed asked.

Alex grinned at him. "I'm great."

———

WHEN HE LEAPED at Eva the minute she walked back through the door, it was *not* to have something to occupy himself so he wouldn't blurt out his feelings. And it definitely *wasn't* to prove that he and Eva were just fine in the sexual department. (Not that he would ever let Will or Bael know that they'd gotten inside Alex's head.)

And when he threw himself at her, she caught him, which would have been hilarious, if they weren't so busy tearing each other's clothes off.

"So was it Zed or Will who said something?" she asked as Alex nibbled down her neck to her collarbone. They were propped against the wall, Eva shucking Alex's pants over his shoulder. Alex was panting when he drew back. He didn't want to answer, but when she gave him that sly, knowing look, he rolled his eyes and chuckled. "It was Bael."

"Really?" She cackled. "I wouldn't have thought he had it in him."

"I didn't think it was all that funny," he muttered against her skin.

"Well, Jillian gave me some pretty good ammo against him tonight, so I'll even things up. Embarrassments galore," she promised as he bit her gently. She hissed, dragging her fingers lightly through his hair.

"You are so the girl for me," he chuckled and then busied himself kissing his way down her neck before he said anything else.

"I see you," she murmured, taking his hand to her mouth. "I see every part of you. And I want it all."

They didn't make it to the bed. And while it was a little uncomfortable, having sex on the hallway floor, their pants made suffi-cient pillows. Alex laid naked on the pine floor, Eva's face pressed into his ribs, nearly asleep. He pulled her against him, relishing the warmth of her against his skin. He pushed her coppery hair back from her face, watching her breathe. He realized he'd been waiting all this time for her to pull away from him. But she accepted him, and she made him feel that acceptance.

He was debating between finding the words to tell Eva he loved her and finding the leg strength to walk to the kitchen for a bottle of water. He really didn't want to tell Eva he loved her for the first time because he didn't have the leg strength to walk to the kitchen. That seemed wrong. Also, he had to stop finding lame reasons for putting it off. He promised himself he would find the right time to tell her, but it wouldn't be with beer on his breath and their clothes thrown around on the floor.

Fortunately, Eva suddenly announced, "So, I think I have a solution to the trucking issue."

"OK, I haven't dated in a while, has trucking talk replaced a cigarette and a nap?" he asked.

"No, I had this idea on the Devil's Armpit night and having sex reminded me," she laughed, nudging his shoulders gently.

"Thank you, I think?" Alex laughed.

"OK, so," she shifted, rolling onto her stomach. "What if you've been thinking of this issue from the wrong angle?"

"Wouldn't be the first time," he admitted.

She sat up and her glorious, rounded breasts at eye level temporarily left him speechless. She rolled her eyes, snickering, her copper hair falling over her face while she pulled a t-shirt over her chest.

"I'm only human," he said, shrugging.

Ignoring him, she asked, "What are we surrounded by here?"

"Grown men who spend inordinate amounts of time taking their pants off during emergency situations?"

Eva tilted her head and stared at him. "Water, smart ass. We're surrounded by water. The Bayou is connected to the Gulf. It's a winding route, sure, but it's there. And if we could set up a connection to the water from a main road in town, it could work."

"Don't you think that would be complicated?" he said. "And we need so much stuff, I don't know if a fleet of boats would put a dent in it."

She shrugged. "I didn't say it would be effective, just that we could tell those trucking companies that we have an alternative, since they're not cooperating. It might make them reconsider their position if they think they're about to lose it. And if you have to sign contracts with multiple trucking companies to achieve the final goal, so be it."

He chewed his lip, thinking. "The exclusive contract was supposed to be a perk for whoever got the deal. I don't know how they're going to respond to having it snatched from under them."

"Well, this way, the lines of shipping stay open and active. And the lack of exclusivity is the price the trucking companies pay for messing around."

"They won't be happy," Alex mused.

"Then they shouldn't mess around," she countered. "There's a large dock, near the edge of town on the Afarpiece Swamp. The local fishermen used to launch charters from there, but people sort of forgot about it because it was just outside the safe zone near the rift, and over the last few years, locals were pretty leery of using it. There are enough spots to dock six boats at a time. Two, if you use large commercial vessels."

He thought about that for a moment. "I don't suppose you would be willing to come work for the League. Help me figure situations like this out when I'm stuck?"

"Oh, hell, no." She kissed him, biting his lip lightly. "You couldn't afford me.

10

———

EVA

EVA RUBBED a hand along Alex's bare back as he slept soundly, face-down in the sheets. She was still having difficulty grasping that this was her life. She had a job she loved and friends she loved and... well, she was clearly on her way to loving Alex, even if she wasn't ready to admit that to him just yet.

She certainly hadn't been ready the day before when the ladies invaded her boat-shop with ice cream and a rainbow of booze in the name of sisterhood. It was clear Sonja and Jillian had been planning this since the moment she took an interest in Alex. This was a Sex Talk Ambush.

Jon had cleared out, the coward, claiming that he had to help Will with "something." She should have known something was up when he didn't go into specifics. Jon loved to "pre-game" repairs, making a plan for how he was going to go about putting an engine back together.

"I don't care how old you are and what species, you're going to need a little post-mortem girl-talk," Jillian informed her as Lia dragged Eva into the house. "And we sent the guys over to spend some time with Alex, so don't worry about him being lonely."

"Do we have to refer to our girl-talk as post-mortem? That makes me uncomfortable," Eva said as Charlotte helped Dani drop onto the sofa. Ingrid handed Dani a pint of Shapeshifting Strawberry Cheesecake and a spoon. Charlotte was already face-deep in a pint of Mystic Mint Chocolate Chip

"That's a good point," Sonja acknowledged plugging in the blender for frozen cocktails.

"So, you and Alex," Ingrid prompted Eva. "Give us the details. He has always seemed that he would be a flexible and generous partner, not too proud to submit to your obviously superior physical prowess."

Eva thought maybe Ingrid was joking, but her expression was completely serious. She really was that frank about all things sexual. Eva supposed she was lucky Ingrid was far more interested in her under-watered tree babies when she'd been fixing the irrigation system. She couldn't imagine what Ingrid could come up with for a captive audience.

"I'm gonna need that booze," Eva told Sonja.

"Coming!" Sonja called back as the blender kicked on.

"Is that what you yelled to Alex?" Ingrid asked.

"Sorry, can't hear you," Eva said over the grind of the blender. Ingrid rolled her eyes and dug into a pint of Fairy-Made Fudge.

Sonja handed her a frosty pink concoction that smelled of pomegranates. Eva winced. "I'm usually not a pomegranate person."

"Just try it," Charlotte said. "And if you don't like it, you can get your beer."

"Thank you," Eva said, sipping the icy drink. It was tart, but not too sweet, and it burned nicely on the way down. "Not bad."

"So, I will put this to you in a much more subtle manner than Ingrid," Cordelia said. "If there is anything you would like to talk about, after your experience with Alex, we're here for you. We know that relationships in the Bayou can be… intense. But don't feel like you have to share. I get that it could be awkward, given that I have a history with Alex."

Eva actually felt her eyes bug out. "I hadn't even thought about that. I'm so sorry, Cordy, this has to be so awkward."

"Honestly, it's not. I'm happy with where I am and with what I have. I'm sort of relieved to see Alex might be happy, too," Cordelia said.

Cordelia was a very nice person and Eva wasn't sure she or Alex deserved her.

Eva nodded. "OK, so 'intense' is a good word for it. I just, I'm... Oh, man, I've never talked to anyone about this stuff before."

"I wasn't used to it, either," Lia told her. "You know that I spent a lot of time alone before moving here. Female friendships are pretty new to me, too. And Cordelia. And it might feel weird, but it can be helpful. And if it's not, we change the subject and talk about the fact that Dani hasn't seen her feet in five weeks."

"If my socks don't match, you are morally obligated to tell me," Dani said, flatly. "Zed thinks it's cute when they're mixed up."

Eva snorted. "It just, it feels different. With Alex? Everything seems to mean more and I'm constantly worried about saying the wrong thing or doing the wrong thing, but then he does something *so* sweet and unexpected and I feel bad for doubting he's capable of that and I think about him... all of the time. Like I could be up to my elbows in a transmission and that's normally a time when I would be laser-focused on what I'm doing, but instead, I'm thinking 'What is Alex doing? Is he thinking about me? Am I going to see him tonight?' And then next thing I know, I drop a heavy metal part on my foot. Fortunately, my feet can withstand a lot. Feelings are nice but they are *super* inconvenient."

Dani pursed her lips. "Wow, when you vent you *really* unload. Good for you."

Eva chuckled into her drink.

"Wait, you've never had feelings for a guy you've been with?" Charlotte asked, her brows raised.

"Well, I'm not a robot," Eva scoffed. "I've liked them just fine, but this is more than a general appreciation... and lust. And it's sort of uncomfortable, but nice. Does that make sense?"

"Yeah, it usually is for a little while – uncomfortable, I mean," Sonja said. "And it's supposed to be if it means something. Otherwise, people would just go around falling in love with everybody. It would be chaos."

"The question is, are you willing to tolerate the discomfort?" Jillian asked. "To get to the good stuff?"

Eva thought about it for a long moment. "I think so."

"I'm glad to hear it," Cordelia said, raising her glass. "It's worth it."

"So, enough about me, what's going on with you all?" Eva asked.

Jillian blinked rapidly. "That is a very candid way to change the subject."

"I have shared all I can," Eva said, downing about half her drink.

There was a long silence.

Sonja repositioned in her seat, clearly uncomfortable. "Um, I have been offered a job with the League's headquarters in DC. It's a big job. Like, 'duties I wouldn't be able to talk about over an unsecured phone line' big. My own department, which I would build from the ground up. And I'm thinking about it. It's too good of an offer to not even consider."

Eva's eyes darted over to Jillian, who didn't seem surprised or alarmed by this announcement. This was clearly something Jillian and Sonja had talked over already. When she noticed Eva staring, Jillian gave a quick upward quirk of her lips into what was not quite a smile. She nodded towards Sonja and Eva refocused her attention on their friend.

The others, however, did not have that kind of restraint.

"What?" Lia practically shouted. "But that would mean moving! And Jon and Will are just now getting closer and that would break Jon's heart to lose Will all over again."

Sonja reached over and took Lia's hand. "I know, I know. Will and Jon are probably going to talk it over today. And trust me when I say that you all and Jon are definitely big factors in our decision, not to mention the clinic and Will's patients and everything we have here. We don't really want to leave. But honestly, when I think about my long-term plans, a job like this is the end goal. I can't *not* think about taking it. It's just something we're talking about."

"And what's going on with you?" Dani asked Jillian, motioning towards her with her spoon.

Jillian swallowed heavily. "What do you mean?"

"Sonja's talking about moving and you're not losing your damned mind? Something's up," Dani told her.

Jillian shrugged. "I am trying my best not to influence her in any way with my selfish desire to keep her where I can get to her."

Charlotte's sleek brow arched. "Bullshit."

"OK, OK, so I may have also received a job offer from the League," Jillian admitted. "They have discovered a new kind of *magique* on a very remote island in Micronesia. The League reps don't know whether they're shifter or fae or something entirely new and they want me to study them. They said they trust me to do so in a non-invasive, non-exploitive manner, which is kind of reassuring that the League is even considering that as part of the equation. It's a huge opportunity."

Eva noted that Sonja didn't respond to this announcement, either. Clearly, Sonja and Jillian had discussed this development in depth. The thought of either woman and their partners moving away struck Eva as deeply sad. She would miss both of them terribly. They were right at the center of this family she'd collected for herself. They were an integral part of it, and while they could carry on without them, there would be pieces missing.

"It would just be a temporary assignment," Jillian said. "We'd come back after a few... years. Bael is willing to take a leave of absence if this is what I want to do. The League could provide support services for the parish in the meantime. And like Sonja, it's too big of an offer not to at least consider it. This would be a significant anthropological event and they're asking me to head it up."

"Have you told Zed?" Dani demanded.

Alex had to know, Eva realized, but he couldn't say anything because this was confidential League business. While she was a little annoyed, she marveled at how difficult it had to be, not being able to tell her about those parts of his job – the parts that would mean a lot to her. Poor Alex. Poor everybody else.

Jillian cringed. "No, Bael wanted me to tell you first so you could be prepared to help Zed through it. We were thinking after the baby is born, so he's distracted."

"Don't use my baby as a distraction," Dani gasped, feigning offense. "Deal with your own life choices!"

"Well, at least we know you and Zed aren't going anywhere," Lia said. "The town would literally collapse if Zed left. No pressure."

"Nah, he loves it," Dani admitted. "Me, too."

"It wouldn't be the end of the world if we moved. There are airplanes that travel to DC, you know," Sonja said.

Dani shrugged. "Eh."

"Also, you're married to a dragon. He can fly you to see our Mystic Bayou family any time you want," Sonja noted.

Jillian shook her head. "OK, yeah, but there's all sorts of dragon-related federal airspace issues to deal with."

"We'll let you know when and if we make our decisions," Sonja said. "But please know this isn't something Jillian and I are taking lightly, and we're definitely taking you all into account."

"You are all major, irreplaceable considerations," Jillian added.

After a few moments, Eva started giggling. "Dragon-related air space issues. This group is so freaking weird."

Sonja scoffed. "You weren't even around for the really weird stuff."

"I don't wanna know," Eva muttered into her glass.

The ladies sipped their drinks (or ate their ice cream), each obviously thinking about how they might be impacted by Jillian's and Sonja's news.

"Anybody else have any fantastic career news that also happens to be emotionally devastating?" Cordelia asked.

"No, I'm remarkably boring," Charlotte said. "Happy, settled.

My biggest problem is that Leonard keeps suggesting extreme sports he wants to try now that he's not cursed anymore."

"My Rob and I are enjoying professional and conjugal bliss," Ingrid said, smiling serenely. "Sometimes simultaneously."

"Somehow I manage to live and work alone with my boyfriend and I still want to see his face every morning," Cordelia marveled. "Oh, and the conjugal bliss thing."

"Well, you'll have to excuse me, but the cub is dancing on my bladder again," Dani said, hauling herself to her feet with some difficulty. She waddled down the hall. "Don't say anything interesting while I'm gone!"

Jillian craned her neck, watching until Dani closed the bathroom door behind her. "Coast's clear."

"OK, I'm really worried about this baby shower that Zed is throwing for Dani," Sonja whispered.

"Really?" Lia raised her hands. "We're going to transition from major life decisions to a baby shower?"

"Wait, Zed's throwing a shower for Dani?" Eva said, shaking her head. "He hasn't said anything about it.

"Yes, he's being all secretive about it," Sonja said, eying the bathroom door. "He wouldn't let me help. And I don't mean, he politely shrugged off my consistent offers of help, I mean, he saw me in my office the other day and when I asked quietly about the shower, he pretended to answer a non-existent call on his cell, said, 'Hi, *maman*, the bees are swarming Mel? Weird!' and basically ran away."

"Yeah, he's mentioned Mel having a bee beard a couple of times," Jillian said, frowning. "It's like he's trying to encourage the universe, or something."

"Dani's really not into the whole shower thing anyway," Cordelia said. "Bonita said something to her about that game where people would measure her belly with toilet paper and Dani actually hissed like an angry cat."

"I think I would do that if anyone tried to measure me with toilet paper," Eva noted.

Jillian added, "At least they're holding it at Clarissa's. She's used to hosting this sort of thing. She has all the tables and crawfish boil equipment already. And Mel's going to love helping her cook."

They heard a flushing noise down the hall, and they all straightened in their seats and acted like they hadn't just been talking about super-secret party plans. Charlotte launched into some story about Leonard trying to juggle on a unicycle and the others pretended that it had been going on for some time.

Eva just shook her head and marveled. Conversations with her birth family had been so volatile, an announcement like Sonja's and Jillian's would have ended in *days* of arguing. Hurt silences. Resentment. But here they were talking about baby showers and hoping for the best.

She liked that, the fact that the people around her took each other's feelings into account, that they took her feelings into account on a regular basis. Yeah, they made weird drinks and invaded her space and asked invasive questions, but they made her feel valued, loved.

Now, in the dark, cuddled next to Alex, she made a mental note to monitor Ingrid's vodka intake during all future get-togethers because she really didn't want to know what a tree nymph considered conjugal bliss.

11

———

ALEX

ALEX AND EVA were curled up on his sofa, having consumed the better part of one of Eva's experimental banana cream pies. They'd pronounced it good, but not *Siobhan good*. And yes, it had taken them two slices each to figure that out.

"I think it was the banana-pudding-to-condensed-milk ratio. It was a little heavy on the milk side. You're going to have to get some more of those Italian biscuits," she sighed, turning her head into the curve of his neck. "Your efforts will be rewarded."

He grinned, snuggling against her. "Well, it's a sacrifice I'm willing to make. For science, you know."

They'd decided to spend the night at his place, because they'd become a little too predictable in their patterns, going to her house every night. If someone was in fact trying to follow Eva, breaking those patterns could only help. If something happened, they would be closer to getting help here than at Eva's remote, but lovely, home. Also, his house smelled like banana cream pie, so it was a win-win.

Alex could only hope Siobhan didn't smell it from across the square, or he would have some explaining to do.

"This is nice," she sighed against his skin.

"Which part? Coming home to someone at the end of the day? Post-pie snuggling? Not having your entire life revolve around work?"

"You brought work home with you," she observed.

"Yeah, but half the amount of work I used to bring home," he protested.

Her giggle was interrupted by the reminder alarm sounding on his phone. He reached over and shut it off without even looking at his phone.

"Isn't that the reminder to call your parents?" she asked. He nodded, threading his fingers through her hair and watching the lamplight dance across the strands as they fell. "But you didn't call them last week or the week before that, either."

He hadn't called his parents since that disastrous conversation with his father, he mused. He'd purposely put it out of his mind, ignoring the alarm every time it went off. He'd pretended it away, focusing on this new domestic bliss he'd found with Eva. It probably wasn't the most mature way to go about it, but... yeah, that was all he had.

"I know this is going to sound really hypocritical coming from me," Eva said. "But is it possible that avoiding calling your parents is just making the problem worse?"

"Sonja says I need to think positive thoughts about my parents if I want to improve my relationship with them. To manifest some sort of response from them, or something."

"Like Zed and the bee beard," Eva conceded.

"Yeah," Alex said, nodding. "Wait, what?"

A heavy knock thundered against his door, the kind of knock that could only come from Zed. And this was a lighter version Alex had asked him to use when his office door had buckled under a bear-mayor's massive fist.

"Come on in, Zed!" Alex said.

They sat up to make themselves presentable. Not because Alex wanted to avoid a brotherly ass-kicking, which he did, but because he honestly didn't want to make the man uncomfortable. Zed put a lot of effort into making sure Eva and everybody else in their circle of friends was safe and happy. Alex didn't want to reward that with pawing at Zed's adoptive sister right in front of his face.

The door swung open and a wall disguised as a man had to duck as he walked into the trailer. He was dressed in worn overalls with leather sleeves and patches at the elbows and knees.

This man was simply enormous. He had to be close to seven feet tall, big enough that Alex actually felt his inner child squeal in terror. The stranger had Eva's nose, long and straight, but with a much heavier brow. His hair was more iron than bronze, and gray streaked heavily through a thick, bushy beard that hung down to his chest. His biceps were covered, but Alex could see they were approximately the size of his head. If this man were to swat a fly with those huge hands, he would probably change weather patterns.

Eva stilled like Lia trapped in headlights. All of the color drained out of her face as her mouth hung slack. Her breathing stuttered and she clutched at Alex's hand.

"Eva?" Alex stood up, edging between this man and his terrified girlfriend. "What is happening?"

All of a sudden, another set of footsteps thudded over Alex's porch and Zed skittered through the open door and around the man – the man who was clearly Eva's father. Zed hustled his frame around the stranger and planted his feet in front of Eva and Alex.

Alex swore his heart grew two sizes. His girl was *loved* here – not just those empty friendship promises people made about helping you move and driving you to the airport, that ultimately fell through. *These* people really would hide a body for Eva. It was possible they already had. He didn't know what they got up to on the weekends.

Why was he having all these thoughts when there was a giant standing in his living room? He couldn't feel his feet. Or his face. Was this what having a cardiac event felt like? This was definitely not the way Alex had hoped his evening would go.

Eva was still clutching his hand as he moved in front of her. He managed to fire enough nerve endings at the same time to squeeze it back.

"Zed?" Eva whispered.

"Heard some guy was asking questions about Eva at the Ice Cream Depot. And Ingrid told him to go fuck himself in tree language," Zed said over his shoulder as he glowered up at the stranger. "When I saw him rushing over here, I figured I should follow."

"My name is Martin Orebender. You have my daughter!" His voice was so low and booming, it felt like an echo through Alex's chest. His accent was strange, more European than Eva's and oddly formal. He sounded like a character out of some medieval movie... about loud, scary men in overalls. "For all their powers and privilege, the League is not allowed to hold us against our will without cause!"

So, Alex had been right, this was Eva's father. When Eva's grip on his hand tightened even more, Alex found his voice. "We're not *holding* her. She's here because she's made her life in this town."

Martin looked Alex up and down with a disdainful glare.

"Why would my daughter make her life in this sad little place? Even for," he paused as if he was holding back a gag, "America, this is dismal."

"Nice people, great pie?" Zed offered. "It's sort of the town's unofficial slogan."

Martin sent him a withering look, and for the first since Alex had met Zed, he looked intimidated.

"Look, even in this 'dismal place,' you can't just kick in someone's door when you feel like yelling at them," Zed told him.

"*That one* told me to come in," Martin noted. "Which speaks to his inability to look after himself or my daughter. Who are you, anyway?"

Alex did not extend his hand for a shake. He knew that was probably rude, but, well, Alex needed his hand and, if he offered it, he wasn't sure he would get it back. Also, Martin had called him "that one," which didn't bode well.

In the most authoritative, calm voice he could muster, Alex said, "I am Alex Lancaster, executive director of League operations in Mystic Bayou. This is my home. Eva is a guest here."

"So that's how you've managed to hide yourself from us for so long," Martin exclaimed. "Doing the League's *bidding* in exchange for their protection? It's one thing to do business with the League, but *this*? You're an Orebender. You must behave as if that matters to you!

Alex didn't like the way her father said the word "bidding," like she was trading illicit favors for anonymity. It was enough to help him find the confidence to bark, "Hold on just one second. Nothing like that is happening here. Eva doesn't work with the League in any way and has received nothing in the way of a special status or protections. And we only started seeing each other recently."

Stepping to Alex's side, Eva squeezed his hand again and shook her head. Alex pinched his lips together. Eva was right. He was giving Martin too much information. The worst thing to do in this sort of situation was to spew words while trying to defend your position. It gave your opponent too much power.

Eva cleared her throat and kept her fingers bound tightly in Alex's as she asked, "What are you doing here, Papa?"

Martin actually looked wounded for a moment, as if he was hurt that Eva would question his arrival. "We've looked for you, every day, since the morning we woke to find you gone, Eva. Why would you think we wouldn't?"

Eva shook her head, as if she didn't believe him. "If this is about the sapphire, I sold it. But I can repay you."

Alex cringed inwardly at Eva's bluntness. Just like this misstep of giving away too much information, it was too early in the conversation to offer that up, in terms of negotiations. And that's all this was, under the bluster and tension – a negotiation. Alex began to relax. He could work with negotiation... even if he didn't entirely believe that Eva sold the sapphire. She hadn't mentioned that when they talked about the contents of her treasure chest. And given the way she talked about her regrets, he wasn't sure she would omit a detail like that. He shook his head. The bottom line was they − he and Eva − needed to know Martin's motivations, what he really wanted and why, before they started offering anything. But this was Eva's father and she was clearly in distress, being in the same room with him.

"Do you think I came here for money?" Martin demanded. "I came here to help you regain your life! Yes, losing the sapphire was a blow to our reputation, our standing in the business, but I can't bear to see you living like this! You're wasting your time and your talent here in this backwater place. You're coming home with me."

Eva let out a huff and Alex could feel her hold on his hand loosening, the blood flowing back into both of their hands as she found her voice. "I'm happy in Mystic Bayou! Doesn't that matter at all to you?"

Martin's thick red eyebrows practically met in the middle as he thundered, "No! Where would you get that idea?"

"You're my father!" she exclaimed.

"Exactly! Your father! And your job as my daughter is to act like you care about your family! You're supposed to use your talents to help us, to promote our interests, our reputation, but you just ran off." Her father made a contempt-filled gesture around the trailer. "For this."

"Yes, *this,* I happen to like this," she shot back.

"A hovel like this hardly compares with the home you fled. You slept in golden halls, treading on floors inlaid with every gem found in the earth," Martin protested. "I cast your bed in solid silver with my own hands."

"Really?" Alex whispered. "What *are* you doing here?"

She nodded. "Not the point."

Alex shrugged. "It's not a *good* point, but it's a point."

"And now look at you," Martin continued. "Your mother would weep to see you sleeping in *prefabricated* housing. No craftsmanship, no commitment. Do you even bother cleaning this place yourself or do you simply throw the disposable house away when it gets dirty?"

"When did you become such a snob, Papa?" Eva asked.

"Much can change in two hundred years," Martin deadpanned.

"I don't actually live here, but that's beside the point," Eva said. "And don't bring Mama into this. Oh, gods, is Mama here, too?"

"No, you may remember we still have a business to run," Martin replied. "Your mother thought it would be better if I came to retrieve you while she kept the workshop going."

The hurt on Eva's face only flashed there for a second, but it was deep. Alex slipped his hand along her waist, just to remind her that he was there with her. She took a deep breath, flashing him a brief smile. "How did you even find me?"

"I do not have to tell you that," Martin huffed. "It's not important how we found you, only that we did."

"It is important if you were the one who sent someone after Eva, running her down in the swamp like some sort of animal in one of those," Zed paused, "what do you call it where the English people wear the red coats and ride horses?"

"Fox hunts," Alex supplied.

"Thank you," Zed said, nodding and turning back to Martin. "Fox hunts."

"You got fox hunts from that?" Eva murmured.

"You spend enough time with him, you start to understand how he thinks," Alex whispered back. "It's a little scary."

"What are you talking about?" Martin demanded. "Who was running you down? Were you hurt?"

"No, my hands are still intact, don't worry," she muttered. "I can still work."

"That's not what I meant – do not speak to your father that way!" Martin thundered, stepping towards her. Zed and Alex moved in unison between Martin and Eva.

"All right, I really appreciate it, but you two have to stop doing that," Eva told them.

"No," they said, again, in unison. Eva snorted.

"You will not keep me from speaking to my daughter," Martin informed them crisply.

"I'd like to see you try to get around us," Alex shot back, making Eva's eyebrows rise.

"How about we just separate for the night? Everybody retreat to our corners?" Zed suggested. "In a day or two, we can all get back to together and talk when we're all a little calmer?"

Martin's mouth turned down in a flustered expression.

Eva groaned. "You don't have a place to stay because you didn't think I would object when you came along and demanded I come home, did you?"

Given the way Martin's brow furrowed, Alex had to guess Eva had it right. And given the housing crunch in Mystic Bayou, Martin wouldn't be able to find so much as a campsite at the RV park down the street. But given the situation, Alex wasn't exactly motivated to help Martin find a place to settle in.

"I will speak to you as soon as possible. We have much to discuss," Martin said, turning and ducking as he left the trailer.

Zed followed him out the door. Alex heard him call, "And in case you didn't pick up on it, when I was saying 'we' over and over before, I was telling you that you won't be meeting with Eva alone. I'm going to be there, and so will Alex, and a couple of other people. Maybe a SWAT team."

Alex shut the door, but left it unlocked for Zed. He turned to Eva, who had sunk into the couch, her eyes wide. "You manifested the wrong parents."

He sat next to her on the couch, "Yeah, sorry about that. You OK?"

"I don't know, honestly." She was staring straight ahead, and he could practically see the gears turning in her head. He couldn't imagine what she was thinking. Sure, his relationship with his parents wasn't great, but he wasn't *afraid* of the prospect of them showing up. And Eva had been afraid and embarrassed, confronted with what she feared in the loudest way possible. He put his arms around her and let her melt against his chest. She exhaled into his shirt. "Thank you."

Seriously, Martin's voice could double for a tornado siren if the town's ever broke. Not that Alex wanted him to stick around.

"So, was it better that your father came instead of your mom, or worse?" he asked.

"Better, believe it or not," she replied. "My dad was always the softer touch."

Alex pulled his head away from hers. "Really?"

She chuckled. "I thought, coming from a family of ironsmiths, that Mama might understand the need to do something different with her skills, to study something new. Jewels weren't exactly her passion when she joined my father in the family business. I mean, I used to find books on blacksmithing in her office, so clearly, she had her own interests. But instead of pursuing it, she sort of doubled down and threw herself into jewelry-making whole-heartedly. Like she had something to prove. So, when I started expressing an interest in mechanics, I thought she would support me. But she told me that this matter was bigger than me, that the family legacy was more important than any one member of that family. I needed to put my dreams aside, any joy I thought I might get from something else. Those thoughts would only make me unhappy. I just needed to put my head down and focus on the work."

He understood that, a heavy legacy you wanted to shrug off. His poor Eva, just trying to find the words she wanted to say to her father but fighting through years of sadness and rejection. He understood that, too. Only he could say what he needed to say to his father. He wasn't afraid, just... tired. Tired of feeling this way, tired of dancing around the fact that his father wanted nothing to do with him, tired of being alone because he was afraid of being rejected before he became a part of something.

He stood, locking the door. He held his hands out to Eva to

help her off the couch. She seemed exhausted, so as she shuffled off to the shower, he got out her pajamas and a glass of water and all but tucked her in.

"I'll be in, just a minute," he said, kissing her forehead.

He walked out to the porch, scanning the horizon carefully for threats or over-sized parents. He called the local security head to tell her to step up patrols of the area near the research village because a large upset man wanted to speak to one of the people staying there. Then he took a deep breath and dialed his dad's phone number.

It took Elliott five rings to pick up this time. "Alex, I told you, your mother looks forward to your calls—"

"And she takes them," Alex interrupted. "She takes them every week and she listens to me talk about my life and she tells me what you're up to. And I don't know if she tells you the things I tell her. I don't know if she even tries because I don't know if you care or not to hear them."

"Now, hold on," Elliott protested.

"No, I've held on long enough," Alex shot back. "Somewhere along the line, I became less important to you than your work. I don't know when or why, but I'm telling you now that I'm not going to try anymore. I'm not going to keep reaching out only for you to let me know that you'd rather be doing anything else than talking to me. I don't deserve it. All I've ever done is work hard to make you proud of me. If you don't like the results, well, that's on you. So, the next step is yours to make. Call, don't call, I don't care anymore, but I'm done letting you hurt me because you don't know how to deal with your feelings."

There was nothing but silence on the other end of the line.

"Nothing to say?" Alex asked.

"I think you've said enough for the both of us," Elliott harrumphed.

"Tell Mom I love her and I'll call her tomorrow," Alex said, and pressed "end."

He rubbed his hand over his face. Well, he'd done it. He didn't know if his dad would ever call him, but at least it would stop hurting so much. He stood, walking through the door and locking it tight behind him. He had to focus on what was right in front of him: keeping Eva safe and keeping her happy. Everything else was just noise.

12

EVA

EVA KNEW she wouldn't have to wait long for her father to find her alone, even with Zed's warning. Martin Orebender wasn't much for letting anyone else give him orders, except for maybe her mother.

Eva was ashamed that she'd frozen so badly when Papa strode into Alex's house like he owned the place. She'd let her guard down, which was stupid considering that she *knew* something was hunting her. But when she was with Alex, she relaxed so deeply, and for the first time in such a long time. And, well, it hadn't helped her at all.

All she could do was stare at his face. He looked a little older, maybe, but much the same. Her long nose, the eyes, the hands. The deep rows in his forehead when he was angry, and he was so angry at her. She watched those lines furrow deeper and deeper as her brain scrambled for the right words. She wanted to apologize, to say she was sorry for taking the stone, that she'd embarrassed him. She wanted to tell him that it had been worth it to her, to make the life that she had, even though she was sure that wasn't what he wanted to hear. She'd never meant to hurt him. That was what she wanted him to know.

But all she could do was react – overreact, really – to every little thing he said because, underneath it all, she was angry, too. Angry that he'd never seen her, angry that he hadn't cared what she wanted, just *angry*. It was such a strange balancing act of emotion, and it left her falling on her face when it mattered. Poor Alex had tried to defend her, which was admirable given the size difference between the two men. But deep down, she knew that when it came to her father, there was no standing in his way. Not when he was trying to get something.

The encounter was a disaster. Everybody walked away without getting what they wanted. Her father without the sapphire and her without closure — if such a thing was possible. So no, it didn't surprise her when she was walking down the street from the grocery store and her father stepped from behind the post office into her path. She refused to let fear show on her face this time, merely nodded at him and tried to pass

"Evalyn, I need a word," Martin rumbled at her.

"I'm sure you need several," she replied. "But Zed was right, we should talk when the League reps are present to prevent any confusion."

"Can you not just speak with your father? Do you really need protectors from *me*? Was I ever so cruel to you?" he asked, his voice crumbling under the weight of grief that fell directly onto her heart. She'd never seen her father so close to crying, not even on the day they entombed her grandmother.

"No," she told him. "And I don't need protection from you, just what you might do. I'm not going back, Papa. I won't ever. I have a life here, one that suits me. I won't give that up."

Martin stared at her for a long time, his jaw working as he processed her words. "I see now that coming here was a mistake. You're too stubborn for your own good, you always have been. I hoped that we could bring you back into the fold. But now." He shook his head as if she'd disappointed him all over again. "Now, I can only warn you."

"Warn me about what?" she asked him carefully, taking a step back.

"As you know, we have been searching for you for some time. And when we couldn't find you, nearly fifty years ago, we hired an outside contractor to track you down and bring you back home. Cost a pretty penny."

Eva hung her head. So, it was true, her parents had sent that creature in the swamp after her to track her down. That horrible creature that made her hear screams inside her head, it was someone her parents thought fit to drag her back under the mountain. Anger, despair, and anxiety all warred in her head.

"What sort of outside contractor?" she asked. "Wait, it's taken him five decades? I mean, I changed my name and all, but I'm not a professional like he is. I'm sure there were times I slipped up. He really couldn't have tracked me down online a little sooner?"

Martin shrugged. "He prefers his ancient methods. I don't think he even owns a car."

"But what about the truck?" she asked.

"What truck?"

"The truck that's been following me all over Mystic Bayou." It was strange to her, that he was acting so surprised. Papa wasn't very good at lying.

"Maybe he rented a vehicle," Martin shrugged. "I don't know."

"So, if you've hired him, call him off!" she insisted. "You know where I am. Take him out of the equation before someone is hurt. He left spikes out on the road for me the other night. Some other person could have driven over them and had a wreck. I care about the people who live here!"

"We've tried. We paid him, years ago, and cancelled the contract. We hoped when we didn't hear anything from him that he'd simply dropped it," he said. "But when he contacted us this week, we realized, it's a matter of reputation to him. He's a hellhound."

Her jaw dropped. "A hellhound? You sent a *hellhound* after me?"

No wonder. Hellhounds were notorious bounty hunters, torment in not-quite-human form. Legend had it that they were once the special pets of demons, sent to drag damned humans to hell for their just reward. But now, they were a little more contemporary. Once a hellhound was hired to find someone, they never stopped looking, and woe to someone who got between the hound and its target.

Someone like Alex, she realized as cold dread flooded her belly. *Alex* could get in the way of the hellhound while he was pursuing Eva.

Hellhounds smelled like sulfur and death. And when they were focused on their prey, if they got anywhere close, the hunted could hear the screams of all of the previous victims of the hellhound in question. The noise was supposed to make it almost impossible for the prey to run due to the fear they were feeling. Her encounters, the dread she'd felt, it was all real. There was a threat to Alex, and it was *real.* And it was all her dad's fault.

"He was very highly recommended," her father said, raising his hands in a helpless gesture.

"Papa!"

"We were desperate, Evalyn."

"I don't get it," she scoffed. "So he knows where I am now. Why not just drive out to my house and get me without all the hellfire and drama?"

Martin sat on a nearby bench and Eva found herself sitting beside him. He sank into a familiar posture, putting his arm around the back of the seat, around her shoulders. It was just as it had been in their home when they were trying to work out a thorny design problem. "I believe he wants to catch you on his own terms. He prides himself on his own cleverness. And according to his reports so far, he's embarrassed at how long you've managed to stay hidden, clever girl that you are. And he can't tolerate that. He likes the chase, the hunt. And I believe you've provided him with a delicious chase indeed."

"I can't believe you did this," she said, shaking her head. "So what's he going to do when he finds me? Finally drag me back home? Keep my head mounted on some sort of creepy display in his den, like a deer?"

"Bringing you back to us, that was the arrangement we made with him when we went to contract, but he seems to be going rogue now, so it's hard to tell."

"Unbelievable." She stood, throwing her bag over her shoulder so hard she was surprised it didn't crash through the post office window.

"I know, it was foolish. We just wanted you back so badly, Eva."

"You wanted the sapphire back," she spat. "You wanted your reputations repaired."

"Just let me help," he said, and it said something about how sorry he was that he didn't get defensive.

"No, you've done enough."

She shook her head, backing away from him.

She didn't run, but it was a near thing. She knew if she ran that Zed would hear about it or one of the others and they would panic. Then again, a little panic was in order because she was being hunted by a *hellhound*.

Growling, she rounded the corner to the research village, where Alex had insisted that she stay until they figured out Martin's plans. To her shock, a black truck – *the* black truck – was parked in front of Alex's trailer. The windows were too heavily tinted for her to see who was behind the wheel, but when she started running towards it, the tires squealed with how quickly it sped away.

"Asshole!" she shouted. She watched as it rocketed down Main Street. There were no license plates on the back, nothing Bael could trace. She turned to Alex's trailer. He'd been so close, just steps from Alex's door. He could have walked right into Alex's home, his office, and dragged him out.

As long as Alex was near her, he was in danger. She'd known that, logically, when she thought she was being hunted. But now that she knew it was a *hellhound?* The bounty hunter could use Alex as bait, or just hurt Alex to distract her, to put her off-kilter so she was easier to capture. That was a feint *worthy* of a hunter, right? Endangering the prey's mate?

Paralyzing dread raced up her limbs, making it that much more difficult to run up the steps. She wasn't sure how she managed to unlock the door with her hands shaking so badly.

She stood in front of the door, grocery bags dropping out of her hands, breathing shallow through her nose. Alex was in danger. No. No. It wasn't tolerable. She couldn't allow it.

There was a way out.

She glanced at the clock over the stove. Alex was at work now. He would be home any minute.

Eva stumbled to the bedroom and jerked her duffel bag out from under their – his bed. She dragged all of her clothes out of the closet, the dresser, the laundry hamper. If she wasn't around, if she could break things off with him, very publicly, so they weren't seen together, he might be safe. He wouldn't be seen as a weakness for her, a soft spot. He wouldn't be hurt.

She zipped the bag over a rumpled mess of clothes and buried her face into a comforter that smelled of him. The only problem was she was going to have to break his heart to do it.

She wanted to be a coward. She wanted to slip out and just never return his calls again, ignore him when he came to her door. She'd done it before, running away, she could do it again, and better. Anything to keep him safe.

She scoured the trailer for any sign that she'd ever been there – hair ties, socks, copies of *Motor Trend*. She didn't want to leave reminders to hurt him. It must have taken her longer than she'd thought because she heard him walking up the porch steps.

"Hey, Eva, honey, we talked about keeping the door locked," he called as he walked through the door and almost tripped over the grocery bags. "What's going on?"

Shit. She was going to have to be such a monster for the next five minutes. She blinked away the tears that were gathering in her eyes.

She could be anything for five minutes if it meant Alex was safe.

Eva breathed in and tried to channel someone she liked not at all, Alex's assistant, Jessica. She slid on her sunglasses, so he wouldn't be able to see exactly how much this was going to hurt them both.

"Sorry, I didn't think you'd be back so soon," she said, working to keep her tone light, disinterested. "I'm just packing up. I'll be out of your hair in a second."

"Wait, what? What are you talking about?" he demanded, dropping his computer bag in the middle of the jumbled groceries.

"Look, Alex, I think we can agree this isn't working out. This was never going to be a long-term thing. It was just, you know, fun," Eva told him. "I mean, you're going to be wrapping things up here in town pretty soon, don't you think? A guy like you isn't going to stay in one position forever. Another League opportunity is going to come up before you know it. Maybe it's for the best we just walk away before things get awkward."

"What are you talking about?" Alex shouted. "I'm not leaving Mystic Bayou and I wouldn't leave you!"

"Oh, come on, we knew this wasn't forever for either one of us." She huffed out an impatient breath. "It's time to move on."

"But you accepted me!" He insisted, taking her elbows in his hands to keep her from moving. "You told me you wanted every part of me. You know how important that was to me."

"And I meant it." She gave an annoyed little jerk of her shoulders and sloughed him off. "At the time."

Steeling herself, she walked toward the door and nearly crumpled to the floor when he grasped desperately at her arm. "Please don't do this, Eva."

"Don't make a big deal out of it, Alex, geez!" she scoffed, jerking away from him and slamming the door behind her. She saw his coworkers crossing the grass, acting as if they weren't watching the woman loudly exiting their boss's home.

Good, the more people who saw, the faster the word would get around. If creepy Man Bun hellhound was skulking around town, he was sure to overhear the gossip.

For good measure, Eva shouted, "It's over!"

She climbed in her truck and drove towards home, though she wasn't sure how. When she reached Jon's place, she turned in to his driveway suddenly and parked the truck. She stumbled out, the engine still running, and collapsed to her knees. She vomited noisily into the grass and burst into tears, long wailing cries that called Jon out of his house. He knelt next to her in the grass, hugging her close as she sobbed.

"I think I did something stupid," she whispered.

He patted her back. "All right, all right. We can fix it."

"That's just it, Jon. I don't think we can."

13

———

EVA

EVA WAS NOT in the mood for a party. She definitely wasn't in the mood for a party celebrating the true love and expanding families of fully grown adults who could manage romantic relationships. But she did love Zed and Dani and she wasn't about to hurt their feelings by skipping the surprise baby shower. Zed had gone to so much trouble for it. He was actually planning to wear real dress clothes instead of one of his "formal t-shirts." So she sucked it up, put on one of her sundresses and a *lot* of undereye concealer, then rode with Jon and Lia to Clarissa's place.

She'd done enough to distance herself from everybody else in the last week or two. It wasn't just a total cut-off from Alex. She'd retreated into the house, not talking to Zed or Jillian, no matter how hard they tried. Lia even tried to arrange a Breakup Rescue Squad to pull her out of her funk. But she'd hugged them and sent them away, vodka and treats unconsumed. The only one she spoke to was Jon and that was because she couldn't figure out how to repair boats from home.

The further she stayed away, the safer her true family would be. But even she had to admit, it was a relief to see them again tonight, just for a night. Surely, it would be all right just to see them every once in a while. She was probably lying to herself, but it was all she had at the moment.

It was obvious something was up the moment they walked through the back gate.

Clarissa's backyard was filled with white matching chairs swathed in filmy bunting. Bael was carrying plates to a huge buffet spread with dumplings, fried pies and all of the other things that Dani had been craving during her pregnancy. The tables centered around a seven-tiered white cake covered in a colorful mix of flowers, which was attracting attention from the bees from Clarissa's hives. Clarissa and a short Asian man with incredibly long fingers were tying bows on a pair of chairs at a table big enough for two near the cake. Well, a table big enough for two, when one of them was Zed.

Clarissa had to stop every few minutes to dab at her eyes, whispering "my *bebe,* getting married to such a sweet girl. They're gonna be *so* happy together."

The *bebe* in question was wearing a white dress shirt and a black jacket and *suit pants.* His hair was tied back with a black leather strip, and he wasn't wearing his usual motorcycle boots. It was the most dressed up she'd ever seen him. He was talking to an older man, wiry and sort of grizzled, wearing a John Deere hat with his suit. Zed appeared to be fetching him a drink and treating him with a deference generally reserved for Clarissa.

Jillian, Sonja, and Will arrived just behind them, and Jillian was so distracted by the site of the party decorations, she ran right into Jon's back.

"Oh, no," Sonja whispered, hugging Eva absently.

"Oh, no, no, no," Jillian wheezed.

"What?" Jon asked as he took the baby from Jillian's arms and jostled Dalinda gently against his shoulder.

Zed came jogging over, a huge smile on his face. "I want y'all to come meet someone."

"Zed, what is this?" Sonja asked.

Zed made a sweeping gesture towards the yard, which Eva had

to admit, looked pretty amazing. "I wanted to do something special for Dani, so I planned a surprise wedding!" Zed said, beaming at them.

Eva's jaw dropped open. She wasn't exactly the one to buy bridal guides on the sly, but even she knew that this was very, very bad.

Jillian blinked at him rapidly. "Oh... no."

Cordelia walked over, wearing a light pink organza dress that looked like something out of a child's beauty pageant. She was carrying a white basket full of multicolored flower petals. Brendan stood behind her, biting his lip as he tried not to laugh.

Cordelia said in a flat voice, "I'm the flower girl." And then she scowled at Eva. "You're lucky you were adopted after the dress ordering deadline."

Eva put her hand on Cordelia's shoulder and patted it sympathetically while Brendan snickered.

"Well, I couldn't make Dalinda the flower girl. She can't even walk yet! I thought it would be cute!" Zed exclaimed, gesturing at Cordelia's flower crown. "And I was *right*. Cordelia looks *adorable*."

Brendan guffawed, bent over at the waist. Cordelia tossed a handful of petals at his face, then growled, "I'm only doing this because I love you, Zed."

"What's happening?" Jon asked. "What's wrong with a surprise wedding?" Jon asked, shrugging.

Lia actually reached up and patted his head while making pitying noises. "I love you, but never, ever do this."

Bael walked over and kissed Jillian. "I know, I know. I didn't have any warning either. I thought I was coming over to help with the kegs. But being the best man, I figured the best course of action was just letting the train roll down the tracks, help out where I can and try to make the best of things when it inevitably plunges into a canyon."

Zed's brow wrinkled in confusion. "What do you mean? This is my big gesture for Dani. I wanted to sell my Harley, but Eva told me to think bigger, so I did."

Jillian turned to Eva, a disappointed expression on her face. Eva raised her hands. "Oh, hey, no, don't pin this on me. Zed, I told you to think smaller! *Smaller!* That's the exact opposite of bigger."

"That's what I thought you said, but when I thought about it, I figured you were trying to use reverse psychology or something. Who ever heard of going smaller on a romantic gesture? That doesn't make any sense."

Eva made a strangled sound. "I meant maybe get her a nice piece of jewelry or a tattoo in her honor or something."

Lia clapped a hand over her face.

"Why does everyone look upset?" Zed asked, his face going chalky under his beard. "Did I do something wrong?"

"Well, in general, a woman likes to have some input in planning her wedding." Sonja kissed his cheek. "You are a sweet, sweet man, but also, sort of a doofus."

Zed looked stricken. "You don't think she's going to like it?"

"Who's that?" Jillian asked, nodding to the older man and the plump, pleasant-looking woman who was helping him into a decorated lawn chair.

"That's Dani's Grandpa Nilsson and her cousin. I-I wanted to make sure her family was here, so her grandpa could walk her down the aisle," Zed said, panic raising the timber of his voice to heretofore unknown octaves.

"Where is Dani right now?" Jillian asked.

"Ingrid and Dr. Assface were in charge of driving her over now. I figured Ingrid would use that blunt honesty to help Dani find the best outfit and make-up and stuff before she left the house. I didn't want her completely ambushed," Zed said.

"That was actually pretty well-reasoned," Sonja said.

"The 'actually' is a little insulting but thank you," Zed replied.

"Also, I thought we agreed you would stop calling him, 'Dr. Assface.'" Jillian noted.

"Surely, there has to be some sort of wedding day exception," Zed scoffed, grinning.

Jillian chuckled and kissed his cheek. "I love you, but sometimes you're just not right."

Around the front of the house, Eva heard a car pull up and honk three times quickly.

"*Le Diable*! That's the signal. She's here," Zed turned to Eva. "Do you think she's gonna hate it?"

"I think all Dani is going to want is to marry you," she told him, hugging him tightly.

Dani came around the corner, wearing a white empire-waisted dress with daisies sewn to the spaghetti straps. Her thick dark hair was tucked up in a braided crown and someone – probably Ingrid – had woven daisies into it. Eva saw the moment that realization dawned on Dani's face, the second that she realized this was her wedding day. Her hands dropped to her enormous belly. Her face was completely blank, and Eva couldn't tell if it was happy-shock or furious-shock.

"Back away slowly," Bael whispered to the others. Zed stepped forward, wringing his huge hands.

Dani laughed nervously. "Zed, honey, what…"

"*Abeille*," Zed murmured, handing her a bouquet of mixed flowers. They were wrapped in yellow ribbon with a little silver bee charm hanging off the ends. "You look real pretty. Um, I did this for you. But I was told that maybe it wasn't the best idea, so if you don't want to get married today, that's all right. We can do it some other day when you've had time to plan."

"Now, I know the girl I raised isn't silly enough to turn down a nice party when it's all set up for her," Dani's grandfather said, poking his head from behind Zed's back.

Dani threw her arms around the man and burst into tears. "Grandpa!"

"Oh, just look at you," Her grandfather said, holding her arms out so he could get a look at her belly. "Your grandma, bless her soul, would have loved to see you all dressed up, marrying your young man. She would have been so pleased to see you with someone who loves you so much, who would work so hard to make you happy."

Reminding Dani of her beloved late grandmother didn't exactly help the crying situation and she sobbed anew. Grandpa Nilsson hugged her close and patted her back. Dani then turned her attention on Zed, throwing her arms around his middle and burying her face in his shirt. Zed looked absolutely panicked and when the Cajun band he'd hired started tuning up for "Here Comes the Bride," he made a cutting motion at his throat. Clarissa swooped in with a handkerchief and patted Dani's hair back into shape. Sonja whipped a packet out of her purse and offered Dani a make-up remover wipe.

"We can fix this," Ingrid assured her. "I snuck your make-up case into my purse."

"When did you do that?" Dani asked.

"I went through your bathroom when you were trying to put your shoes on," Ingrid said, making Dani's eyes go wide. "I had at least twenty minutes."

"See? All sorted. Now, how about you go freshen up real quick and we'll get you two hitched?" Grandpa suggested gently. Dani nodded, wiping quickly at her cheeks.

"OK, I love you," Dani sniffed to Zed and then kissed him.

"I love you something awful, darlin," he replied.

"Nice save, Grandpa Nilsson," Bael whispered as Sonja, Jillian, Clarissa, and Cordelia rushed Dani into the house. Eva stayed with Zed, where she thought she might be needed to haul him off the ground. He looked like he might pass out from relief.

"Probably should leave the big surprises alone for a while, son," Grandpa told Zed softly. "Birthdays, weekend getaways, that sort of thing."

"Noted, sir," Zed agreed, watching Dani waddle into the house.

———

In the fifteen minutes it took Dani to fix her make-up, the other guests arrived and filled the empty chairs under Clarissa's watchful eye. Unfortunately, those guests included Alex, who sat in one of the back rows and studiously avoided eye contact. She supposed that he only attended because it would look bad if the head of League operations didn't attend an event thrown by the Mayor. But just once, Eva wished Alex would leave an obligation unmet so she could have some peace.

Dani made it down the aisle on her grandpa's arm, both absolutely beaming. Her cousin, Trudy, had been ordained over the internet so she could preside over the ceremony – something that had made Dani laugh so hard it had interrupted the service for five straight minutes. Eva watched her friends exchange their vows, and for a moment, she forgot about hellhounds and her own family issues. She just basked in the glow of two people who knew what they wanted in life and had found it.

As Zed wept his way through the "I do's," Eva glanced towards Alex. Her only comfort in this emotionally tumultuous situation was that he looked just as miserable as she was, practically slumped in his seat, wrinkling his suit. She turned in her chair and it was all she could do not to fold in on herself, too.

Something inside of her was broken and she didn't know how to fix it. She looked around at this beautiful celebration and didn't think she would ever have something like this. She wasn't sure she wanted it, because it wouldn't be with Alex. He would move on to some other town, or some other woman and she would be left to what... watching him fall in love with someone else?

She forced herself to look away, disguising a full body shudder as Trudy got to the part about objections. Zed glared at the guests as if he would go full grizzly on anyone who dared.

Eva wanted to scream. She wanted to jump to her feet and run to Alex and tell him she was sorry, that she didn't mean it and she was only trying to protect him. She wanted to tell him they would figure out some other way to keep him safe, but that she couldn't be apart from him anymore. She wanted to tell him that she missed him, that she woke up every morning thinking about him and went to sleep each night missing him. She wanted him to know that she heard he'd implemented her plan for the dock, that it was almost ready to use and that she was happy she could help him, that he respected her enough to trust her ideas.

No.

You will sit still and focus on your friends and their happiness, she told herself. *You will not burst into noisy, snotty tears. You will put Alex's safety ahead of your feelings. You will paste a smile on your face and have some dignity. And then you can go home and get rip-roaring-selkie-level drunk and then fall asleep face-down in your couch.*

She nodded sharply.

Right. Good plan.

Despite her friends' attempts to draw her into the festivities, Eva kept to the edge of the party, watching. After the cake was cut, she decided she needed to leave before she embarrassed herself. Rob and Ingrid were leaving early, because "weddings put Ingrid in the mood" and offered to drive her home. Eva approached the bridal couple to say goodbye. Dani was sitting with her feet propped in Zed's lap while he fed her buttercream.

"Don't get up," Eva told Dani, kissing her cheek. Zed rose to hug her one last time. "You throw a hell of a wedding, Zed. It was beautiful."

"Wasn't it?" Dani sighed. "I could pout about being left out of the planning, but he pretty much did everything I would have wanted − including inviting my family − and I didn't have to stress out over it. So, it was a win-win."

"I'm so glad, *abeille*," Zed sighed. "For a second there, I thought I'd really messed up."

Over Dani's shoulder, Eva could see Alex leaving the reception early. He'd made his official appearance and now he could retreat.

"I didn't expect it to hurt so much," she whispered.

"That's how you know it's love, *cher*," Zed told her softly. "Just tell him. Take it from someone who damn near lost the love of his life from sheer stubborn stupidity, it hurts less when you just tell them how you feel."

She shrugged, even while it felt like the weight of the world was pinned to her shoulders. "You're sweet, but I don't think that's going to work for me. Enjoy the honeymoon."

Zed wriggled his eyebrows.

On the drive home, Eva was for once grateful for her distress, because it distracted her from the comments Ingrid made about her plans for Rob once they dropped Eva off. That woman was lovely, but she had *no* filter. Eva stared through the window, into the darkness, wondering how many more events like this she would have to face in the future. She should have known better, thinking that she could keep her distance from him. Maybe Alex would move along to some other assignment? Would she have to leave the home she'd built, the family she'd made? Was that preferable to seeing him?

She really didn't know.

But when she arrived home, Eva's father was sitting on the porch of her house, waiting patiently. She did not expect that. What did he want from her? Hadn't they already had their awkward follow-up conversation when he told her that he'd sent a monster after her? What more was there to say?

"Um, should I call someone?" Rob asked. "Because that guy is kind of large."

"It's just my father," Eva said.

"But I thought that was a bad thing," Ingrid said. "I thought your father issued a contract on your head because of your dishonest handling of the family business assets."

"Ingrid, sweetheart, that's one of those things we talked about, softening the language a little bit?" Rob whispered.

"Am I wrong?" Ingrid asked, her brow furrowed.

"No," Eva assured her, patting her shoulder. "You're not wrong. And it's fine."

"Are you sure you're OK?" Rob asked as she climbed out of the car.

"I should be *fine*," Eva promised.

"All right, but I'm texting Bael," Rob told her.

"That would be nice. Tell him my dad will be leaving shortly," Eva replied. "Thanks for the ride."

Ingrid took the hand still resting on her shoulder and leveled Eva with a look. "Sometimes, we have to forgive ourselves for the things we have done wrong before we can expect other people to forgive us."

Eva blinked, startled by this helpful insight from Ingrid's usually... acidic brand of conversation. "Thank you."

Ingrid smiled. "Come to the shop tomorrow, if you want to talk. I have just made a large batch of mocha chocolate chip."

"Thanks," Eva told her before shutting the car door. She straightened her shoulders, taking a deep breath as she approached Martin.

"What do you want, Papa?"

Her father crossed his arms across his chest. "Is that really how you're going to greet me from here on?"

"I don't know how else to talk to you," she retorted. She thought about what she'd wished she'd said in Alex's trailer, on the bench on Main Street. And then she began, "I spent years running from you because I was convinced you could never forgive me, not just for taking the stone but because I hurt your precious reputation. Do you know what that's like? To know that you matter less than what other people think of your family? You *set a hellhound* on your own daughter because you couldn't bear that people might think you were weak or foolish. That thing could have killed me and it was worth it to you!"

"I realize that was a mistake," he said. "I was hurt when we issued that contract, Eva. My pride was singed. And seeing you now, I realized how wrong I was, not just in calling in the hellhound, but what I expected from you, what I thought I deserved from you. I didn't realize how different you would be, out here, in the world. You never had that spark in your smile, at the table with the loupe over your eyes. Seeing you with that light in your face, I can't believe I lived so long without it."

Eva didn't know whether to trust him. It was more than she ever hoped for, these words from her father. And it just seemed too easy that he would say them to her without her telling him everything.

"You never hurt me, not back then," she told him. "You just never saw me. You refused to, and I think that's what hurt the most."

She braced herself for the angry roar, for him to tell her that she was ungrateful and spiteful, but all he did was nod. "You're right. I spent a lot of years upset with you, hurt by what you did. And I think that's why we were desperate to get you back. It wasn't about the stone."

"I think for Mama, it was."

"Well, maybe for Mama. But we both wanted answers, too. And when we didn't get them, we lashed out," he said. "But seeing you now, you're happy here. And even though I said didn't care... after seeing it with my own eyes, I don't want to take that away from you, no matter what it does to my reputation."

"What about Mama?"

Martin pulled his lips back into a grimace. "Well, that's going to be a hard sell. She's still angry and hurt, but I don't think we're going to be able to fix it without talking," he said. He offered her a smile, not quite the broad grin of her childhood, but more than she'd expected from him. "And I hear you're very good at fixing things."

She nodded, speechless and still as he awkwardly wound his long arms around her and hugged her. She could smell what used to be home on his shirt, smoke and copper, and she squeezed him back. "I missed you," she told him. "I made a life without you, and it's a good life. But I missed you."

"We missed you, too," Martin said. "Not just for your skills, but because we missed *you*. The den is too quiet, without you around."

"Too free of dropped tools and colorful cursing, you mean," she snorted.

"Well, I missed the cursing. Your cousin Gerta isn't nearly as creative as you are with the obscene adverbs," he told her.

"Wait here." She ducked into the house and pulled the chest from under her bed. She retrieved a small wooden box from under the compartment where she kept her pick-axe. The box was ornately cast out of silver, a coming-of-age gift from the aforementioned cousin Gerta. She jogged back to the door, afraid for a moment that she would come back to find her father gone.

But he was still there, waiting, when she extended her arm and pressed the box into his hand. His jaw dropped when he opened the box and found the Ocean's Eye, glittering in the moonlight. "I thought you used the proceeds to live..."

She shook her head. "I said that to make you sweat, which I know wasn't very mature of me. Hell, I didn't even admit to Alex that I still had it. It was hard enough admitting that I stole it in the first place. But really, I couldn't bear to sell it, even when things were so lean I barely ate. Somehow, I knew that I should return it someday. I just didn't know how."

Martin swallowed thickly. "Thank you. We forgave you, without your returning it, but this goes a long way in easing the hurt feelings, I think."

"I'm not sorry."

Martin gasped, "Eva!"

There it was, the explosion she'd been dreading, but all Martin did was laugh. And that gave her the courage to say, "I'm not! I'm not sorry that I left. I'm not sorry that I went after what I wanted, when you wouldn't even listen to me. But I suppose, I am sorry that I stole from you. That was wrong, which was why I never sold the sapphire. It wasn't mine to sell. But it was the only way I could show you how serious I was about leaving. I hadn't considered that you would chase me down for it."

"You didn't think we would chase you?" he exclaimed, still chuckling. "You're our daughter!"

"You told me you didn't care about my happiness!" she shot

back.

"Well, that doesn't mean I don't care about *you*!" he cried. "I would like to see you again sometime, if that's all right with you."

She smiled and nodded. "You know where to find me."

"Goodnight, my jewel," he said.

"It's a little soon for that," she told him. "But goodnight, Papa."

He looked sad when she said that, but he still waited for her to close the door before he left. Some instincts, she supposed, never changed.

She walked inside, shaking her head at this strange new development. A lot was changing all at once and it didn't exactly reduce her urge to drink the better part of a bottle of scotch. She slipped out of her party dress and into a pair of running leggings and a tank top. She wanted to be comfortably dressed when she got fall-down drunk. No one wanted to pass out in skinny jeans.

She had just poured her first tumbler – OK, it was a red Solo cup, but still – when her cell phone rang. Alex's number showed up on her screen. And while a small thrill of relief coursed through her, commanding her hands to pick up the phone and hear what he had to say, she hit "ignore." It would hurt too much, to talk to him. She was too raw from the conversation with her father to deal with the mistakes she'd made with Alex.

She raised the cup to her lips and was about to indulge in that first sip when the phone rang again. Another call from Alex. She hit ignore again, only for the phone to flicker back on in seconds with Alex's number on the screen. She closed her eyes and swiped her thumb across the screen. "Alex, please, I'm trying to–"

"I don't give a shit what you're trying to do," a harsh voice barked out of the receiver. "But Alex here wants you to shut up and listen."

Eva froze, dropping her cup. "Alex?" she yelled. "Are you there? Who is this?"

"I'm the hound that's been chasing you all around town, you half-wit. And if you don't be quiet, I'm going to start peeling parts off Alex and mailing them to you, one by one."

Her breath stuttered out in a panicked wheeze. Alex. The hound *had* Alex, which really pissed her off. "I can't be too much of a half-wit if you haven't caught up to me," she shot back. "Leave my friends out of it. They've done nothing to you."

"No, you just hide behind your asshole friends to protect you. You haven't been alone once!" he shouted. "And then this little twerp started hanging around, and it took me even more time to assess his connection to the League. But now I know he's harmless – just another low-level lackey, and a *human* at that. Hardly worth my time..."

In the background, Eva heard Alex yelp. "Eva, he's crazy! Just stay away!"

"OK, stop, stop. Don't hurt him. We're not even together anymore," Eva yelled. "Just let him go."

"Well, if you're not together anymore, why would you care?" the hellhound scoffed.

"Because I'm not psycho! Just because we're not dating doesn't mean I want to get pieces of him in the mail!" she cried. "Look, I've just given my father what he wants. He said he called the contract off and I'm willing to pay you whatever was left of your fee if it's unpaid. Hell, I'll pay you for your trouble if you'll just leave town."

"I don't give a shit about your father or that damn sapphire!" Man Bun barked. "This isn't about a contract anymore. It's about *my reputation.* You've damn near ruined mine and I won't have it! You will meet me at that shitty makeshift dock at the edge of town. You will not call the police. You will do that within the next fifteen minutes. Because if you don't, I'll kill him. I have nothing to lose anymore."

"Eva! No!" Alex shouted in the background. "Go to Bael, go somewhere crowded. Just stay away! Stay safe!

"Alex!"

Man Bun's voice echoed in her ear before the phone line died. "Drive fast."

14

EVA

EVA WASN'T A COMPLETE IDIOT. She had no intention of driving out to the dock alone without telling someone where she was going. This hellhound was unhinged and there was no telling what he'd do to her if she surrendered. The best-case scenario was that he'd drag her back to her ancestral home, which would be both awkward and a huge pain in the ass. Then there was the worst-case scenario, that he'd kill her and she'd end up in the afore-mentioned taxidermy display. And she really didn't want to give him that opportunity. At least, not without a hell of a fight. Unfortunately, her friends were still so busy at the wedding that no one was picking up their cell phones. She left messages with Bael, Jillian, Sonja, Jon, anyone she could think of that might be able to send back-up.

She was weirdly calm as she charged through the house, reached under her bed for the treasure chest and then ran for the door. She didn't even bother locking the chest or hiding it. She wasn't sure if she locked the door behind her. She didn't care if she walked into the house and found every jewel missing.

Alex was in danger.

Eva didn't remember driving across town. She could only think in terms of the terror and dread she'd felt when the hellhound chased her down the road. Was Alex feeling that now? Was it worse than what she'd experienced because he was closer to the hellhound?

Her breath caught in her chest as she barreled down Main Street. What if Man Bun hurt Alex anyway? What if he wanted her to show up and find him dead because he knew it would demoralize her? Alex could die, believing that she didn't care about him, that she was just the latest person to tell him that he wasn't enough. He could die believing she didn't love him.

Thinking of finding him injured, bleeding, Eva mashed her foot down on the gas, practically swerving off the gravel road. She didn't notice any other cars around, but she hoped that maybe someone would see her speeding through town and call Bael. But when she arrived at the darkened dock, she didn't have help. She only had herself, and a giant fucking pick-axe.

Because like it or not, she was an Orebender, and she had to use the weapons she had at her disposal.

Eva scanned the shadows as she threw the truck into park. There was no sign of anyone else, not even another vehicle – that didn't exactly make her feel better. She climbed out of the truck, weighing the axe handle in her hands and listening. That same feeling of being watched crept up her spine like cold fingers. She refused to hear the now-familiar screams, even as a single bulb clicked on over the dock. She was about to separate that asshole from his man bun. Forcibly.

Eva squinted, her eyes adjusting to the sudden invasion of light. Alex had implemented her ideas! She could already see the bare bones of a rudimentary shipping facility – the beginnings of slips, lighting, signs. More importantly, she could see a rusted dark red shipping container, barely balanced on the end of the dock, with its doors open. And inside was a man, sitting in a folding chair. The low light glinted off chains wrapped around his chest.

Alex shook his head, his words muffled by the bandana tied around his mouth. It was blue, printed with pouting stars.

"Alex!" she yelled, gripping the pick-axe as she ran forward.

He'd used one of her own bandanas to gag her boyfriend. That just added insult to injury.

"Ah-ah-ah." That awful gravelly voice scraped against her eardrums as a hulking dark-haired man melted out of the shadows and walked into her path. He was built like a bulldog, all barrel chest and short, almost bowed legs. He wore Ray-Ban sunglasses, despite the dark hour.

"Who the fuck are you?" she demanded.

This was not the creep she'd yelled at in the grocery store. This was an entirely new creep.

"I told you, I'm the man your family sent to fetch you," he said. "It took me long enough, following your scent from one pointless corner of this country to the other. But here you are."

Eva's tense shoulders dropped. "I owe Man Bun an incredible apology."

"What?" the man demanded.

"Nothing," she said, glancing at Alex, who was struggling to wriggle out of the chains. Eva took a deep breath, but those screams grew louder in her ears, as if people were running down a tunnel towards her.

"Gods, that's awful," she said, shuddering.

He smirked at her. "That's the terror that fuels me to my next challenge. And your screams are going to be the sweetest of all, just because you've pissed me off."

"Look, Hound, can I call you 'hound?'" she asked, feigning the confidence that she needed to get through this conversation.

"My name is Kip," he grumbled.

"Really? OK," she said, shaking her head. "My dad and I are good. I know you're pissed, but there's no point in this whole thing. Just let Alex go, then you and I can talk through this. He's not essential to this conversation."

She attempted to circle around him, towards Alex, but Kip stopped her. "Not so fast."

"I told you, I'll pay you," Eva said, circling in the other direction. Kip growled, whipping off his sunglasses. The screams were so loud that Eva dropped to her knees. The axe landed next to her with a clang.

"This isn't about money," he growled, his voice dropping to a demonic depth. "I told you, this is about reputation. I've chased you for the better part of fifty years. A hellhound, the underworld's greatest hunter, and I can't catch some spoiled girl on the run from her family!"

She grunted, forcing her way to her feet and dragging the pick-axe with her. She glared at him while he monologued, barely paying attention to her. Until she moved toward Alex, and he kicked out at her. She dodged, rolling to the side, struggling to move under the weight of those tortured screams.

"I don't care if you've made up with your idiot parents," he seethed. "I don't even care about getting paid at this point. I signed a contract to deliver you to their home, as soon as I managed to capture you, and that's what I'm gonna do. You *will* join your boyfriend in that container over there. You two will be shipped on the closest transatlantic freighter going to Europe. There's supplies and water enough for *one* of you to survive the journey. I'm sure you'll make that choice easily enough. And then I'm gonna take a picture of you, bound and trussed like a Thanksgiving goddamn turkey on your parents' doorstep, have it developed and print it out for everyone to see. So everybody knows I'm still the best!"

"Really, you still take photos to the developer?" she asked, shaking her head. "Are you using one of those cardboard instant cameras, too?"

"Yeah, what's wrong with that?" he demanded.

"Nothing, it's just going to be hard to do that," she panted, pushing to her feet again. "With a pick-axe lodged in your fucking skull."

"Oh, please, little girl," Kip sighed, turning that awful fiery gaze on her again. She clapped her hands to her ears, dropping her axe. But she managed to stay on her feet. "You're not even a challenge for me."

In the distance, another scream sounded, higher and sadder, like the howl of desperate grieving. Was that another hellhound? Did these guys hunt in pairs? Eva hoped that they didn't because screams from two of them might make her head explode.

Kip tilted his head, distracted. The screams from his eyes stopped and Eva could breathe again. The grieving cry stopped and silence hung in the humid air for a moment before it was followed by the roar of a bear and the beat of a dragon's wings.

That hadn't been the screams of another hellhound, she realized. That was the cry of a banshee.

She laughed, praying that whatever death Brendan was predicting, it wasn't Alex's.

"What is that?" Kip growled.

"You're so screwed," she laughed. "I might be a spoiled little girl. But you're nothing compared to a pissed-off bear. And you just interrupted his honeymoon."

"What?"

While Kip was distracted, Eva slid the axe handle through her hands like a pool cue, smacking him broadside across his manly forehead. He howled, transforming into a huge smoke-grey hound, like no other dog she'd ever seen, all teeth and claws and flaming eyes the color of nightmares. He snapped at her, nearly catching her arm in his razor-sharp teeth. She pivoted, crashing the handle end down on his toes.

Despite herself, she just couldn't find it in herself to seriously injure a dog. Kip barked and knocked Eva backwards into the water. Her axe sank to the bottom, but it was forgotten as a herd of mismatched shifters thundered over the horizon.

Her family had arrived.

Climbing onto the dock, Eva realized that she hadn't seen them in their shifter forms all at once, but it was pretty damn impressive seeing them arrive like that. Kip charged forward, clearly displeased at his territory being invaded.

An enormous brown bear topped the hill, roaring and stomping his feet. Quicker on her hooves, a golden deer skidded to a halt, sending a spray of dirt into Kip's face. When he dashed in to snap at her, Lia raised her flashing front hooves, only to have a flaming blue phoenix cross between them, sending Kip scuttling back. Eva pushed her way onto the dock, only to feel it shake underneath her. Bael's huge green-and-gold dragon form had landed near the dock with a deafening bellow, shaking the ground.

Eva's head whipped towards the shipping container which was wobbling off the end of the dock. "No, no, no!"

The metal box tipped at a weird angle, closing the doors. It was as if some unseen underwater hand was yanking the corner under the surface. It bobbed up sharply and then began slipping down. Eva's sharp ears could hear water pouring inside through the space between the doors.

The container was sinking, with Alex inside.

"Alex!" she shrieked, then ran down the dock, diving into the water headlong. Behind her, some sort of battle was raging, but she couldn't hear it with the water rushing into her ears.

In inky water, she could barely make out the shape of the container sinking through the bubbles. How was the bayou this deep? Her eyes adjusted as she kicked down to the doors. Fighting the changing water pressure, she reached through them and pried them apart with all her strength. The rusted metal groaned as it tore like tissue paper in her hands. Water rushed over her, filling the remaining air space left in the container.

Alex was bound to a folding chair, which was chained to the floor. His eyes were wide with panic as he struggled against the chains. She struggled to kick downward as the container sank. Alex seemed to keep moving out of her grasp, no matter how fast she moved.

After a few agonizing seconds, she closed her fingers around his arm, pulling herself level with him. He shook his head, nodding toward the opening of the container, as if she would abandon him, as if she would just leave him there to drown and save herself. Rolling her eyes ever so slightly, she reached down and yanked at the chains, which had been welded with much stronger metal than the stupid doors. And she was trying to avoid hurting him.

He kept making hand motions that Eva interpreted as "go away and save yourself." She pulled herself to him and covered his lips with her own. She still had some breath in her lungs, and she gladly shared it with him. She wasn't sure it would work, but she had to *try*. His kiss was desperate, like he was trying to memorize her mouth. Reluctantly, she moved away, sliding down his body and returning to the chains.

It took several strong yanks before she was finally able to pry open the loop securing him to the container floor. Her lungs burned with the instinct to take in air, but she had to ignore it. If she sucked in water, she would drown. At this point, she wasn't even sure which way she should swim to reach the surface. Fortunately, Alex seemed to know. His hand wrapped around hers and he kicked, pulling her upwards with him and out the doors.

She was so tired and it was taking all of her concentration not to breathe in. The edges of her vision blurred and turned gray, and it seemed so much easier just to slip off into sleep. But there was Alex's hand, cold and slippery, twined in hers. Her head bobbed under the weight of keeping herself conscious, but then something pale moving through the water caught her eye.

It was a... fish... with Jon's face. Was she hallucinating because her brain was running out of oxygen? No, wait, there was another one, just behind Jon's fish that looked like a fish with Will's face.

No, that was Jon was in his shifter form, which was honestly not too different than his human form. Other than sharp teeth, hyper-extended cheekbones, and a strange sleek gray tail from the waist-down.

Weird.

"Don't worry, sweetheart, I got you," Jon's voice sounded inside her head in a strange echo. He was swimming at her so fast that her fading eyes could barely keep up. It felt like she'd only blinked and Jon had his arm around her waist, rocketing her upward toward the dim light. She shook her head weakly, grabbing towards Alex, but

Will already had him in a similar hold. The Carmody brothers had their heads above water in another blink and Eva sucked in air with a rattling wheeze.

Next to her, Alex spluttered and coughed. Whatever fight had happened while they were drowning, it was over. Zed was in human form, stepping into a pair of sweatpants. Bael was hiding in the brush because apparently his pants were a casualty of battle. Lia and Jillian – wearing over-sized t-shirts that Eva suspected belonged to Zed – were so busy laughing that they were of no help.

"It's good to have mermen friends," Eva sighed.

"Deep breaths," Will said, shifting back to his human form. "Don't panic now. We've got you."

Alex shrugged Will off gently, then wrapped his arms around Eva. He clutched her to his chest so tight that it hurt. But she wasn't about to complain about it.

"Did either of you breathe in any water?" Will asked.

Alex shook his head. "Nope, and it was a real fight, let me tell you. And *you*." He turned on Eva. "Don't you ever do anything like that again!"

"Save you from certain death?" she asked, sagging against Jon as the Carmody brothers towed them to shore.

"Yes!" Alex shouted. "You breathed your last bit of air into my lungs. You keep your breath where it belongs, keeping you alive."

"It's my breath and I'll do whatever I want with it," she retorted, with as much dignity as someone being towed through the water like a toddler could manage. "And also, how often do you expect to get into 'certain death' situations?"

"Well, lately, it feels like we get into them about every six to eight months," Jillian muttered.

"Here, I brought a backup pair, just in case," Brendan said, tossing them to Bael. "I was permanently scarred by seeing Zed's junk in our last fight-to-the-death."

"I will not be ashamed of my body!" Zed crowed with a little hip shimmy.

"Where's Kip?" Eva demanded, scrambling up the bank to her feet.

Alex collapsed on the ground. "I'll be up in a minute. I'm just going to lay here until I can feel my legs. Also, who's Kip?"

"The hellhound," Eva said.

"Really?" Jon asked, tilting his head. "His name is Kip the hellhound?"

"Oh, then he's zip-tied and locked in Brendan's trunk," Lia said. "It was easy enough after Bael smacked him with his tail. Knocked him right out."

"He was chewing on my spare pants – and the leg they were tied around – at the time," Bael grumbled, emerging from the brush in his borrowed pants. "I don't feel right about it."

Alex sat up, looked around, and then sank back down to the ground. "Wait, if no one died, why did Brendan scream?"

"It was a fake scream, an intimidation tactic," Brendan admitted. "I don't bring much else to the table, except for driving the containment car."

"As soon as I can get up, we can take him to the League's holding cell," Alex said from the ground. Eva slid down next to him and propped his head in her lap. He yelled, "I'm gonna remember that smack on the back of my head, asshole!"

"He can't hear you, honey," Eva told him.

"I would claim that he wouldn't have gotten the drop on me without the element of surprise, but I think we all know that's not true," Alex muttered, nuzzling Eva's leg.

"Come on." She chuckled and scooped him off the ground bridal style. "Will's gonna put you on oxygen."

"Sure the hell am," Will said. "And tetanus shots for everybody."

"I would say I don't need bottled air, but my girlfriend is carrying me like a baby because I can't support my own weight," Alex said. "I don't mind, though. Did you see her rip the doors off the container? Sexiest damn thing I ever saw."

"Yeah, buddy, I saw it," Will promised.

"Can we get a cat?" Alex asked Eva. "I think we should get a cat. We can name him Ted."

"Oh, you're going to be so much fun until your brain is fully oxygenated." Jon laughed, patting Alex's shoulder.

"We'll drop by later, but we better be getting back to Clarissa's," Jillian said. "It took Cordelia, Sonja, *and* Trudy to hold Dani down on a chair while we were leaving. Her grandpa finally had to use guilt and cake to keep her from coming down here and zapping... Kip."

"Such a lame super-villain name," Jon muttered.

Eva waved her hands wildly and exclaimed. "Right?"

———

CONTRARY TO WILL'S PROMISE, it turned out Eva didn't need a tetanus shot. But Alex did get the promised oxygen. Sitting next to his bedside, holding his hand as Will examined him, Eva fully grasped how close she came to losing him and it made her heart hurt. She thought about all the days ahead of her, a seemingly endless stretch of empty time without Alex making her laugh, making her feel the only real warmth she'd ever felt. The very idea was terrifying. She'd been foolish and she'd been afraid, and that fear had almost cost her everything.

She'd lived in fear for years, and it had turned out that while, yes, her parents had been angry with her, if she'd just given them time to calm down and talked to them – maybe she could have saved herself some years half-lived. But then again, she wouldn't have become the person she was now, and she liked the life she'd built and the person she'd become, the person Alex loved. She wouldn't have the family she'd built, the people who chose her and loved her for who she was. They'd seen through the lies she'd told and seen the person underneath and loved her anyway.

Eva had almost ruined all that. She wouldn't do that again.

"Well, you escaped pretty much unscathed, but I'd like to keep an eye on you for the next few hours," Will told Alex. "Eva, I'm leaving you in charge of him. If he makes any stupid decisions, like standing up, you have my permission to take him out at the knees." Alex snorted. "That's weird advice from the guy who just spent thirty minutes making

sure I was healthy."

"I like to keep busy," Will retorted as he walked out of the hospital room.

Alex chuckled, squeezing Eva's fingers lightly. "It's a little embarrassing, that he barely had to look at you to know that you're just fine. Stupid human brain and body that needs more oxygen than yours."

"I happen to like your human brain and body," she told him, kissing the hand free of an IV drip. "I'm sorry. I'm so sorry that I hurt you. It came from a place of love–"

He objected quietly, "That didn't mean it hurt any less, Eva."

"I know, I know. I hurt you because I was trying to protect you, yes, but I was also trying to protect myself from the pain of losing you. And all I ended up doing was hurting both of us," she said.

"Well, you haven't exactly cornered the market on making bad decisions rooted in fear," he told her. "I've been so afraid of not being enough for you, I wasn't enough for you. I should have listened more; I should have seen more. I should have seen how scared you were, and I should have helped. I was so ready to give up that my foot was half out the door at the first sign of trouble. I was trying to protect myself, too. I should have worried more about protecting you."

"From myself?" she asked.

"If necessary," he said, grinning. "I don't know about you, but I'm so tired of being afraid."

Eva nodded, blinking through the tears burning in her eyes. She leaned down and kissed him, then again. "Me, too."

"And I'm tired of living without you," he added. "And not just the last few weeks. I mean, I'm tired of living any place that doesn't have you in it. I don't think you'll want to move into my trailer, but it seems presumptuous to invite myself to move into your place."

"I'll have you packed up and moved in before you get out of here," she promised.

"Will says I don't have to stay overnight," Alex reminded her.

"I know people who get shit done." Eva said.

"Ah, yes, your terrifying but loving family," Alex said, chuckling.

"They're your family, too," she protested. "They didn't just show up for me. They showed up for you. I called them and told them you were in danger, and they came to help *you*. Don't forget that."

Alex's grin was crooked as his eyes grew heavy. "They did, didn't they?"

15

———

ALEX

ALEX HAD NEVER HOSTED anything at his home and, given the amount of work involved, he wasn't sure how he felt about it. But Eva was so happy, putting around the house – their house now – getting everything ready, that he couldn't argue with her.

Speaking of the lady of the manor, Eva was lifting a chest-sized cooler under one arm, careful not to tip the ice and beer out as she moved it onto the porch. Alex stood at the grill, watching her lift it effortlessly, and swallowed. He would never get used to living with someone who could do those things. It was strangely arousing. And it was going to be really embarrassing if everybody showed up to find him sporting a tent beneath his *"Kiss the Cook"* apron.

"It's like I'm sleeping with a superhero," he marveled.

"Technically, you're cohabitating with a superhero," she said, giving his mouth a smacking kiss. "And I think that makes you the Lois Lane in this scenario."

Alex considered it, pursing his lips. "I will make myself a little 'Press' badge and embrace it."

Ted the cat, a tabby rescue – who was female, thank you very much – wound her way around Alex's ankles. Ted had moved in the same day Alex had been released from the clinic and moved his belongings into Eva's house. She'd accepted him *telling* her that he was moving back in with her and living there forever with surprising grace, but nearly losing him to a waterlogged shipping container had been enough to convince her that living apart was a little silly. Her father... was not thrilled, but Alex didn't know whether it was because Eva was staying in Mystic Bayou or because she was staying there, living with a human.

Alex had received a surprise visit from Martin before he'd been released from the clinic. It had been disturbing to wake up to a seven-foot-tall man looming over his hospital bed, but he'd managed not to make any noises that were too embarrassing. He had to hold on to that tiny remainder of his dignity.

"So, you're courting her, little man?" Martin had rumbled.

Alex had swallowed around the enormous ball of fear lodged in his throat. "If she says I'm courting her, I am. I'm just glad she lets me anywhere near her."

"What have you offered her?" Martin asked, his eyes narrowed.

"My devotion and respect? Also, rare and extremely-difficult-to-find pie ingredients." Alex said.

Damn his oxygen-deprived brain! He spoke to intimidating people *for a living.* Why couldn't he pull it together right now?

Martin scoffed. "She's an Orebender. You present her with a proper courting gift, or it is an insult to our way of life and her craftsmanship. She deserves nothing less than her weight in copper. Or topaz. She was always partial to topaz."

"I will keep that in mind."

"You will keep that in *her accounts,*" Martin told him. "Or you will hear it from me."

With that, Martin had stood and walked to the door, pausing only to say, "She's a good girl. Special. She deserves someone who appreciates her for who she is."

Martin had promised to come back with her mother – *invited,* this time – when Eva was ready for a visit. Alex was hoping that Eva would wait a while to issue an invitation, but he wouldn't keep her from asking them. Lord knew she was going to have enough to put up with when his own parents came to visit – *if* his parents ever came to visit. His own mother had called to let him know that she'd given Elliott a piece of her mind when he'd come home, blustering about Alex's "nerve" to talk to him the way he had. She'd announced to Elliott that they were retiring, and *she* was choosing where. And since she'd handled their finances for the last forty years... Elliott had no choice but to agree. She'd let Alex know where they landed and would try to talk him into a visit by Christmas. Elliott was not going to like any of these developments, so he doubted the visit would be very pleasant.

What if they all decided to visit at the same time?

Alex suppressed a shudder.

Still, Alex was sort of looking forward to having someone around who could tower over Zed. That would be fun to watch.

"You're going to want to try to finish the grilling before Zed and Bael get here because they will supervise every move you make," Eva told him.

Alex nodded. "I know I made a big deal about being accepted in the friendship circle, but have we considered if this friendship thing is really worth it?"

"Get to grilling," she told him.

"All right, then."

Their guests sort of crashed into the house like an ocean wave, loud and all-encompassing. Jon and Lia were the first to arrive, carrying an enormous number of side dishes and a really large pick-axe, the one she'd shown him the night he'd seen her jewel collection. Alex vaguely remembered her carrying it with her the night she heroically saved his ass.

"You found it!" Eva exclaimed, throwing her arms around Jon. "Thank you!"

"Well, it's the benefit of not having to breath underwater. You can find stuff," Jon said, clearly pleased that he'd made Eva happy.

"Thanks, man," Alex murmured as Eva looked over the freshly cleaned axe.

"Anything for her," Jon told him. "And by extension, you. Just remember that."

"Still getting used to the idea," Alex said.

Jon's answer was drowned out when Ingrid and Rob arrived with a carrier bag filled with pints in all flavors from the Ice Cream Depot. For their contribution, Cordelia and Brendan brought several boxes from the pie shop. Alex knew that Brendan had shown up for him, when he was in danger, and it did quite a bit to dispel the last of the awkwardness between him and Cordelia. They were grown-ups now, for the most part, in grown up relationships with people they cherished. There was no reason they shouldn't try to be friends now.

Sonja and Will contributed more beer and a medical bag because, as Will said, "You just never know." Bael and Jillian hopped out as soon as they arrived to try to prevent a car ride-based baby tantrum that would inevitably lead to flames. Zed and Dani were the last to arrive, with Charlotte in tow, as Dani was due to deliver at any minute. Leonard followed with Charlotte's midwife bag and a drop-cloth to protect Eva's furniture.

Alex was still trying to adjust to the idea that they weren't just here to see Eva, they were here to see him, too. That they valued him, saw him as worthy of their legendary group efforts. It was still amazing to him. He didn't quite know what to make of this new family, but that was all right; they knew how to take care of him until he figured it out.

It felt like a mad scramble, trying to make sure everybody had a drink, a comfortable place to sit (in Dani's case), and enough fridge space (for the backup beer), but the great thing about her − their, he corrected himself, *their* family − was that they made themselves at home without being invasive about it. And they helped out rather than waiting to be served.

"Well, I still feel bad about the Man Bun guy," Eva was telling Sonja. "It turns out he was just new in town and was trying to ask me out."

"No, staring intensely at someone in public and following her home is an extremely questionable approach to courtship," Sonja assured her.

"How are your parents settling in at the research village?" Sonja asked Lia as she helped her arrange the side-dishes on the counter. As more League employees moved out of the village, Alex had decided to designate a handful of trailers as space for visiting "dignitaries." Considering that Darwin Messina was literally salivating to work with Mr. Doe as a business consultant, Lia's parents were definitely qualified.

"Well, the trailer's not up to my mother's standards, of course," Lia said, rolling her eyes. "But I'm glad they're here because I think it will encourage her not to visit again. But my dad loves it. He's already gone on multiple runs in the woods, said he's never seen so much wild space in one place."

"Or they could follow my parents' lead and retire here."

Lia turned pale. "That's not funny, Sonja."

"So your parents have officially decided on settling here?" Dani asked, running a hand over her belly. Lia sank into the nearest chair while Jon mixed her a strong cocktail.

"Yeah, that brings us to a couple of announcements," Sonja said, grinning at Will. He slid his arm around her waist and kissed her temple. "So we've officially decided to turn down the job offer from the League. Our life is here, Will's patients, you all. We can't just move away from all that, from our home. Maybe someday, if things change, if you're not all here together, we'll think about it again. But for right now, we're not going anywhere. We've even put in an offer to buy the *maison* from the town."

"Which I've already approved," Zed announced, lifting his beer bottle in a toast. "Nepotism has its privileges."

Alex clapped a hand over his face. "Please don't say things like that in front of me. It just creates paperwork."

"Hey, it counts for you, too," Zed assured him. "You won't let me lick your forehead, but you're just as unofficially adopted as Eva."

"I won't let you lick my forehead because one, it's gross, and two, that would make me Eva's unofficial sibling," Alex protested. "And that makes me uncomfortable."

"Well, I'm gonna keep trying to get your forehead when you're not looking," Zed informed him.

"Oh, come on, Zed, last time you poked me in the eye, and it really hurt," Alex cried.

"Well, stop trying to dodge, then!" Zed exclaimed.

Sonja snickered. "Well, with the nepotism in place, my parents are going to build a little cottage on the edge of the property so they're close enough for us to help as they get older."

"But far enough away that we all have some space," Will added. "We're following the Zed and Clarissa model."

Zed chuckled. "Wait until the first time Sonja's *maman* walks into the house unannounced on No-Pants Wednesday. And then we'll talk."

"What is your life?" Bael asked Zed, shaking his head.

"Oh, thank goodness," Jillian cried, clutching Sonja to her. "But are you sure? I'm thrilled you want to stay but I don't want you to give up your dream job and regret it."

"I gave it all due consideration," Sonja promised. "There was a lot to gain. A lot. I mean, the insurance coverage alone."

Will cleared his throat. "Sweetheart."

"Not the point," she conceded. "But there was so much more to lose."

"And on that note, I don't feel weird announcing that Bael and I have decided that we're not going to Micronesia," Jillian said. "As tempting as the offer is, I can't represent the needs of Mystic Bayou's locals from another hemisphere. There's just too much happening here. I unleashed this genie bottle on the town, and I can't just leave you to deal with them while I waltz off to bigger things. And you're here and Mel is here and everybody we love."

Jillian smiled up at Bael, who pressed his forehead to hers. "This is home. Besides, I've already had my significant anthropological moment in my career. Let someone else have a turn."

"To some things, the *good* things, staying the same. Dammit, we deserve some of that after the last few years!" Zed crowed, raising his bottle. The rest of the group cheered.

"Charlotte's new clinic on wheels is up and running," Leonard blurted out, beaming at his girlfriend. "She's practically overrun with patients. We're going to have a regular baby boom here in town."

"I may have to call my mom in as back-up," Charlotte said. "Which would be horrifying and hilarious, in terms of no-pants interruptions."

Leonard's smile disappeared. "What?"

"And if we're making announcements," Alex said, clearing his throat. "At this week's board meeting, I'm going to be presenting a press release officially revealing Mystic Bayou as the location of Jillian's report. Zed's already read it, but he wants approval from Jillian and Sonja before we move forward."

"Are we sure that's wise?" Bael asked, holding Dalinda close to his chest.

"Wise? Who knows? But definitely necessary," Zed said, his face growing more serious. "If Mystic Bayou is going to live up to what we've said about it, how we feel about it, it's got to open to everybody. I'm not going to say it will be easy, but it's necessary. It's gonna take all of us." He leveled a look at Eva and Jon and Lia and anyone else in the room whose facial expression read something along the lines of "how am I going to be of any use?"

"All of us," Zed said again. "Because, yeah, it's scary, but each one of us has faced something a lot scarier than zoning problems and transportation issues and a lack of parking on Main Street. And people who want to write a check at the grocery store, I mean, it's the digital age!"

Dani cleared her throat. "Sweetie, focus."

"We've faced far worse, and we've done it together," Zed said. "And that's how we're going to do this."

"Very inspiring," Bael said, smirking at him.

"Oh, shut up, Bael," Zed barked, chucking a deviled egg at him. The baby sent out a cloud of blue flame that incinerated the egg mid-air. The room went silent as the baby scream-laughed. Even Bael looked slightly disturbed.

"Our baby's not going to be able to do that, right?" Dani whispered, eking out a long, slow breath.

Zed shook his head, never looking away from the tiny pile of egg ashes on the kitchen floor. "I don't think so."

"Good," Dani said, inhaling deeply. "Because I'm pretty sure that my water just broke."

Alex froze. He had no idea what do. Staying silent and not making any sudden movements seemed like a really good plan. Eva only laughed, slipping her hand into his and squeezing it gently.

"Told you the drop cloth was a good idea," Leonard crowed, raising his arms in triumph.

"I'm very happy for you," Dani told him, snorting.

"OK." Charlotte stood, clapping her hands. "We've prepared for this, people. This is Plan Delta, Variation Six. Follow the plan. Get to the clinic."

"Plan?" Zed wheezed. "What plan?"

"From page twenty-six of the book," Charlotte assured him as Sonja and Jillian sprang into action, gathering Dani's belongings and carrying them out to the car as Bael helped Dani to her feet.

"There was a *book?*" Zed demanded, breathing heavily along with his wife.

Alex was never more grateful for the existence of a book.

Charlotte placed her hands on Zed's cheeks and gave him a smile. "Mr. Mayor, look at baby Dalinda. I helped bring her into the world and there was a giant metal egg and a dragon involved. By comparison, your cub is going to be a breeze. Now, breathe with me."

Zed inhaled through flared nostrils.

"OK, Zed, breathe out."

Zed turned a dark crimson.

"Zed," Charlotte nudged him.

Bael smacked his oxygen-deprived friend on the back. Zed took a deep, gulping breath.

"I'll drive," Bael told Charlotte.

She nodded. "That's a good idea."

"I think I should go as back-up," Will told Eva, kissing her cheek. "Not for Dani, but for Zed when he inevitably loses consciousness."

"You're a good man," Eva told him, making him grin. "We'll come by the clinic when you give us the all-clear."

Leonard took Dalinda in his arms and shouldered her diaper bag. "We shouldn't mention to Jillian that Bael left the baby behind. Just seems like a bad idea."

Alex put his arm around Eva's shoulders as half of their guests ran out the door. "Kind of a weird way to end our evening."

"Not with us," Jon replied.

Eva laughed, watching the cars peeling out of their driveway. "I kind of love it."

Alex kissed her, tucking his hand around her jaw. "I do, too."

They watched the brake lights disappear into the growing twilight, knowing that the night ahead of them, the months ahead of them, were going to be difficult and chaotic. But it was just like Zed said, all of them would have to face it together. Because it was important. Because it was what they had to do to keep their family together. Because it was what they had to do to make other people feel just as safe, just as welcome.

Because Mystic Bayou was home.

THE END

ACKNOWLEDGMENTS

I am eternally grateful to the readers and listeners who have embraced Mystic Bayou and its characters. Thank you, as ever, to the fantastic Jonathan Davis and the voice in my head, the incomparable Amanda Ronconi, for bringing this cast of characters to life. I learned so much from Wayne Keyser, host of "Ballycast," and thank him for permission to use terms listed in the Ultimate Carny Lingo Compendium, which I found to be an invaluable source of information. Louisiana State University and Cajunradio.org provided the resources I needed regarding Cajun French phrases and pronunciations. I am so happy to have Brenda Rosen's *The Mythical Creatures Bible*, along with Emma SanCartier's *Monsters You Should Know,* as part of my research library. They provided inspiration for some of the strange creatures shown throughout this series. And to Rose and Natanya, thank you so much for your endless support and patience.

****all lists are in reading order****

The Southern Eclectic Series (contemporary women's fiction)

Save a Truck, Ride a Redneck (prequel novella)

Sweet Tea and Sympathy

Peachy Flippin' Keen (novella)

Ain't She a Peach?

A Few Pecans Short of a Pie

Gimme Some Sugar

The Mystic Bayou Series (paranormal romance)

How to Date Your Dragon

Love and Other Wild Things

Even Tree Nymphs Get the Blues

Selkies Are a Girl's Best Friend

Always Be My Banshee

A Farewell to Charms

The "Sorcery and Society" Series (young adult fantasy)

Changeling

Fledgling

Calling

The "Nice Girls" Series (paranormal romance)

Nice Girls Don't Have Fangs

Nice Girls Don't Date Dead Men

Nice Girls Don't Live Forever

Nice Girls Don't Bite Their Neighbors

Half-Moon Hollow Series (paranormal romance)

The Care and Feeding of Stray Vampires

Driving Mr. Dead

Undead Sublet (A story in The Undead in My Bed anthology)

A Witch's Handbook of Kisses and Curses

I'm Dreaming of an Undead Christmas

The Dangers of Dating a Rebound Vampire

The Single Undead Moms Club

Fangs for the Memories

Where the Wild Things Bite

Big Vamp on Campus

Accidental Sire

Peace, Blood and Understanding

Nice Werewolves Don't Bite Vampires

The "Naked Werewolf" Series (paranormal romance)

How to Flirt with a Naked Werewolf

The Art of Seducing a Naked Werewolf

How to Run with a Naked Werewolf

The "Bluegrass" Series (contemporary romance)

My Bluegrass Baby

Rhythm and Bluegrass

Snow Falling on Bluegrass

Standalone Titles

And One Last Thing

Better Homes and Hauntings

Pasties and Poor Decisions (in the *I Loved You First* anthology)

ABOUT THE AUTHOR

Molly Harper is the author of more than thirty paranormal contemporary romance, women's fiction, and young adult titles, including the Half-Moon Hollow series, the Southern Eclectic series, the Sorcery and Society series, and the Audible Original Mystic Bayou series. Molly lives in Michigan with her family.

Where to find Molly
Website: https://www.mollyharper.com/
Twitter: @mollyharperauth

photo credit: J NASH PHOTOGRAPHY

 facebook.com/Molly-Harper-Author-138734162865557

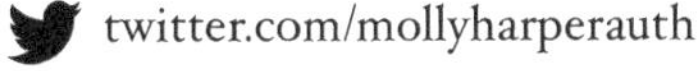 twitter.com/mollyharperauth

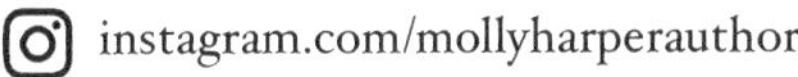 instagram.com/mollyharperauthor